BEYOND THE UNKNOWN CULTURE

A Cross-Cultural Journey to Ethnic People
Beyond Our Comfort Zone

Don Heckman

Table of Contents

Introduction

This book will examine this and other fantastic stories: Each story is a mirror of the heart. A nomadic Tuareg pilgrim to Mecca came to me and asked for more and more stories from the Bible. He was trained in Quranic verses. I wondered how he would allow me to share openly with him in a Western cultural form. Yet, as a storyteller, I was able to enter into his oral tradition world. He kept saying, "Don, tell me more stories from the Bible."

The working title of this book was "TWO THINGS YOU CAN TAKE WITH YOU TO HEAVEN." The working title of this novel is clearly a mystery that stirs up questions. The Nigerians have a great proverb. "The hearse that drives your dead body to the cemetery does not have a roof rack on top." The poor and the rich can't take much with them to their eternity, with two exceptions. You can take yourself and the person whom you lead to Christ to heaven. This book is an accompaniment to the church seminars that I have conducted across the world, mainly in the USA. It is also more in-depth than a 2-day or 3-day seminar and fills hundreds of areas that could not be addressed with time limitations.

The book has true stories with real places and events that did happen exactly as they were described, though it is a novel, so names can be changed. Interwoven into the elements of cross-cultural ministry are stories that are true and intentional to show how the forces of the world, religions, and darkness are working cross-culturally against us to undo all the work of the Lord in which we engage. Such attacks seek to make us avoid intercultural, cross-cultural, and enculturation constructed, which really is not optional but determinative for our spiritual lives and our Christian existence.

Chapter 1

This novel presents insight and examples which come straight from the numerous cross-cultural seminars which I have presented in cities, states, and nations that you may have attended. These seminars are an open the door to reaching people of any and all ethnic backgrounds. Right now, many Christians are a silent body of speechless and fearful, and ill-equipped religious people who have sometimes become introspective and unable to cross cultures to fulfill the last command of Jesus Christ, which is to reach every ethnic people and nation in Jesus' name.

A Dental Appointment Changed My World and a Whole Church

We need to start with my dentist here in France. I needed nine crowns, three root canals, and two new bridges. Ok, the young dentists down the road into the town of Bonne gave me an estimate of $18,000. They had all the latest equipment and machines, and yet I called them the children, since they looked straight out of dentistry school. I went online, as most of us do. I looked into prices in India, Israel, Thailand, and Turkey. I found that one of our associate missionaries in Izmir, Turkey knew a Christian and fabulous American dentist in Izmir, Turkey. So I called the dentist and received a warm welcome and booked for two weeks with the dentist. I found an Airbnb for $10 per night. The bill ended up costing me $1,200. But wait, this wasn't the best part. I told the dentist,

Vincent, that I wanted to go to a Turkish church on Sunday. That is where everything took a huge turn.

The Turkish church was to start at 1:30 pm. It was next to the British Embassy to make it look like the Islamic country of Turkey tolerates Christian worship. I sat on the grass outside. I waited until 3:00 pm. No one came to church. A kind woman approached me and said that the members of the church were on a retreat that Sunday in the forest with other believers and would not be in church at all. I looked at this lady who proposed an alternative. She said there was another church three blocks away. It was near the car wash. But she knew nothing about that church.

I walked into the scorching heat and asked for the car wash. Three people told me that car washes don't operate on Sundays. I said, OK, just tell me where the car wash is situated. I found two things. First that the church was being locked up since it was now 3:30 pm, and I had to make a crucial decision. Second, the church was an Iranian church with all the believers having been converted in Iran. The next step was pivotal.

I said to the six elders who were locking up the church: Stop! Unlock the church! I have a special word for you. I shouted this out forcefully. They opened the padlocks, and the doors and put on the air conditioning and the lights. We sat down in a circle with translation from my English to three who only spoke Farsi, the Iranian language. My word to them was that I knew in the Lord that they were downcast and totally saddened by some event or circumstance. I read the word the Lord gave me from the Bible. It was Psalm 44. I read the entire Psalm where the Israelites totally obeyed the Lord in every way, however, the Lord not only did not respond to them, but God let enemies attack them without end. I explained how this church called Church of the Resurrection was in the same situation as the Israelites and knew no response from the Lord in Psalm 44. The Lord, I interpreted the Psalm, is not like a Coca-Cola machine, where you put in a few coins and out comes the drink. If we expect certain acts of obedience or worship will obligate God to do our bidding, we are short of understanding since we are not going to manipulate the Lord. Rather, I urged, whether the Lord reveals His will to the elders or to the church or not, we are called to strongly praise Him, to be empowered to give all our strength to Him, and to turn from sadness to shouts of worship and a renewal of God's unanswered plans without settling for despair. Give the Lord your best and turn from mourning to shouts of praise. Immediately the six elders stood to their feet and said that the Lord had spoken, and now we are ready to walk in power and renewed faith like never before.

The part that I never knew that this church was the church of Andrew Brunson, who languished in prison, arrested by the Turks for evangelizing everywhere. The next service was to start at 6:00 pm. Word of my explanation of Psalms 44 went through this church of 200 as it was whispered all around, and power and joy caught on like a raging fire. I just was used by the Lord in a way that the Iranian elders launched a powerful proclamation to the whole church in a way that was God's hidden way. Members of the church came up to me to offer me food, Starbucks coffee, translation, and huge thanks. What was the result? The visiting pastor saw the power of God so visible all around. He made an altar call after he preached. He called for those willing to disciple and live with new converts for three months, teaching them the power of reaching out, knowing the Word, becoming flames of light, and doing this as they housed themselves with new converts day and night for 90 days. Fully 100 people came forward to the platform and committed to this very radical formation and transformation of new converts into power houses for the Lord. Four more altar calls were given, one to care for and feed the disciplers, another to commit to endless prayer, another to commit financially to the disciplers who had bills to pay, and another for those who were going to keep praying for Pastor Andrew Brunson, who is now free from years in prison. People were weeping in church, praising God, on their knees, and literally revived and renewed and lifting up their voices for the privilege of knowing Jesus and serving Him.

Chapter 2

Enculturation Is The Theme Of The Iranian Church

Jesus' mission to the Samaritan woman includes a process of "**enculturation**"; not only because it takes place in the Samaritan people's territory, which was despised by the Jews, but also because it is a witness to by a person who is a woman and a Samaritan who overflows with witness to others. This explains why the disciples, firmly locked into their being Jews, were unable to invite any Samaritans to encounter Jesus at the well. The text's emphasis on this aspect invites us to develop Jesus' ability to reach out to others and transcend differences and prejudices. Enculturation is the bringing of a person of another culture to Christ that changes others. The Samaritan woman told the whole town in a way that all the town's people came to Jesus, as Jesus "leveraged" one person's witness experience.

These disciples had not understood why Jesus was talking to the Samaritan woman or what he wanted of her (John 4:27), and so they were invited to see what is already happening around them. Along with them, readers of the gospel are invited to transcend the limitations of human divisions and marginalization in order to see and understand the image of the "fields already white for harvest": the Samaritan people who are on their way to Jesus at the well because of the witness that the woman has given to them (4:29-30). Now, the legitimacy and appropriateness of

Jesus' behavior in "violating" social customs become clear.

Enculturation includes helping converts to accept their native cultures so they can influence other non-Christians to come to Christ within that culture. Teach Muslim converts to accept interacting and enculturation with Muslims, for example.

Conversion is not an excuse to form a club that rejects other Muslims, for example or any other home culture. Many Muslim converts become anti-Muslims instead of committed to loving their Muslim friends and family. Teach and show Muslim converts to love other Muslims just as you do. Also, Muslim converts sometimes reject new Muslim converts. Due to the high price that most Muslims pay (nothing compared to the price that Jesus paid), the tendency is for them to set the bar very high for new converts. This can lead to harshness as Muslim converts deal with other new Muslim converts. MBBs, Muslim Background Believers, should love and encourage new converts who are weak or sinful in some area, and not reject them.

Let me introduce another enculturation incident. Mohand was a North African who had given his life to serve, honor, and obey the philosopher Nietzsche, who said that God is dead. He arrived in France and went to a church that threw him out because he looked non-European and was considered a threat and a terrorist. He came to the Muslim convert church that I planted and joined us on our day of fasting. He carried a sack lunch to the event. So he was curious. After speaking with him dozens of times, Monhand said he could not break his vow to Nietzsche. I was exasperated. Finally, I just put my arm around him and said that I loved him. With that act of love, he walked around the city of Paris for 7 hours as God showed him the love of the Father. He gave his life to Jesus. I was elated. But there is more. The enculturation event happened as he went out to share Jesus with another friend. Mohand came to me and said, Don, you are a grandfather. I was confused. He said that I was his spiritual father and that he led another friend to Christ, making me a spiritual grandfather. More astonishing was the news that Leysin, the man he led to Christ, was traveling in the metro when a man fell dead on the train. Leysin only knew that Jesus was the way, the truth, and the life. To the amazement of everyone on the train, Leysin prayed for the dead man who jumped up alive, well, and totally healed from death. This is enculturation, as one person leads still another to Christ.

Chapter 3

Ahmed is a Muslim friend Whom God Loves

Most Non-Western Cultures Are Shame/Honor Cultures, Not Guilt/Sin/Repentance Cultures: We Have To Find Out "Which" structure is evident here as we cross into another culture

Ahmed had a family of six children in Algeria. His wife announced to him early one morning that she was pregnant with his seventh child. Ahmed was already partially paralyzed on his left side. He couldn't till the soil and work the fields due to his paralysis. That meant that he couldn't possibly feed and provide for a seventh child on top of the six others.

Ahmed couldn't bear this shame. In fact, the shame was so great that Ahmed decided at once to commit suicide. Ahmed took a pistol with him to a coffee bar, where he decided to drink his last coffee. When he finished the espresso, he put the cup down and prepared to shoot himself.

But things didn't go as planned. By God's grace, a Christian came into the coffee bar with a baffling background. He was a man like Jonah of the Old Testament, unwilling to serve God but doing it anyway. This reluctant Christian said to God, "OK, I'll take these Gospels of Luke to this coffee bar, though it is probably for a lost cause!" (We have since met this "former Jonah-type," who is now a zealot for Christ).

The Jonah-like Christian gave Ahmed a Gospel of Luke and left. Ahmed read part of the story of the Prodigal Son. This is the story of the Jewish father that was shamed but still loved his son. Ahmed trembled. He went home. His wife cried for joy because she saw that Ahmed was still alive, he hadn't followed through with his plan. But Ahmed said, "Woman, leave me alone! I have a book to read."

Ahmed read the Gospel of Luke, the book of the Bible most suited for Muslims since it speaks of Samaritan honor, prodigal dishonor, and other shame and honor themes. Ahmed gave himself over to God, and over a period of three months, he was miraculously healed of the paralysis in his left leg! Ahmed plants churches today.

This is the usual start for Muslim evangelization: Most often, Muslims are told that either God has a wonderful plan for their lives or that Jesus Christ, the Son of God, died for their sins. But the greatest perceived need of Muslims today is not the assurance of salvation for their sins but deliverance from being in a nearly constant state of defilement or shame. Freedom in Christ from defilement is another way of describing salvation. A better consideration for evangelization: Tell them the story of Adam and Eve. Tell them that Adam and Eve were created without shame. They sinned and had to hide from their shame and defilement. Our Muslim convert church in Paris is led by an Algerian convert who came to Christ by reading the story of Adam and Eve in the Garden of Eden after they sinned. That's right! He said that while Adam and Eve were defiled and living in shame, God never left them. God called for them, He clothed them, He corrected them, He gave a promise to them, and He kept them alive.

Muslims have never heard that God associates with or dialogues with, cherishes, and even loves defiled people. In fact, the greatest form of blasphemy in Islam is the concept of "syirik," that God seeks out and cares for defiled people because (for them) it diminishes God's greatness as being removed from humanity. As Muslims say, Allah-U-Akbar, or God is great, which Muslims also take to mean we are worthless. But in Christ, Ahmed went from "worthless and defiled" to useful and valuable to Christ.

Chapter 4

Compare Cross-Cultural Activity With Intercultural Action

Since a cross-cultural approach to mission work has reinforced divisions between cultures, an intercultural approach to mission is encouraged. Unlike cross-cultural interactions, in which both parties can separate and return to their respective cultures with little change, intercultural interaction changes both of those involved so that they become a new culture. Intercultural interactions are driven by the desire to form lasting relationships. In a collaborative team process, as an example, it was demonstrated that an individual's understanding of terms such as collaboration, team, and community had been influenced by cultural assumptions. To prevent our cultural assumptions from becoming a barrier, we must work with those of other cultures to forge a new set of cultural values. Can you imagine doing "cross-culture" work and finding out that we have become changed as well as the person with whom we speak?

Mission work, by its very nature, involves culture crossing. Paul pointed out, "how can they believe in him whom they've not heard? How can they hear unless someone is sent." He further outlined the necessity of adapting to the mission field culture in 1 Corinthians 9, "I have become all things to all people so that I might save some." While mission work across cultures is not new, today, we stand at the door of unprecedented opportunities to meet unreached people internationally and domestically. The bringing of the Gospel is an opportunity due to the large influx of immigrants into the United States and other Western nations. This includes all countries of the world where people are in motion and transitioning, from war-torn nations, from poverty, or just to increase their earnings to the dream of a more significant income.

The challenge with cross-cultural interactions is that we settle for accommodation rather than embracing transformation in intercultural interactions. All mission work is cross-cultural in nature. We go overseas and eat the food, listen to the music, and hear their stories, but we always cling to our culture and process the experience through our culture. We allow ethnic ministries to use our facilities. We may, on occasion, share a worship experience in which some of their music is played, and some of our music is played. Some of the worship is in their language, and some of it is in our language. We may have a potluck where we may try some of their food to be polite, and they may try ours so as not to be rude. Notice that the differences are tolerated rather than celebrated. There is a clearly defined line between them and us.

The Apostle Paul affirmed that cultures and peoples would find Jesus in their cultures. Acts 17:26-27 reads, "So that they should seek God, in the hope that they might feel after him and find him, although he is not far from each one of us." Is Paul trying to contextualize the gospel? Is he contextualizing culture as a path to the gospel? More than ever, I see Paul himself becoming contextualized, if you will, by finding a place in his heart for people of very different beliefs. I am all for contextualization. But much of the talk about contextualizing the gospel for Muslims forget that it is incumbent upon us to open our hearts wider to people, not just to find a place for *dishdasha* robes and *salat* prayer rituals in a Christian context.

Community life will radicalize Western missionaries or other cross-cultural workers. What we know about community as Westerners needs to be re-examined to understand where and how non-Westerners live. Many cultures have keys to the Kingdom of God already within their cultural expression called the *Umma*. *Umma* is an Arabic word that means "community of believers," a deeper meaning of community when compared to what we know in the West.

The most powerful example of public, oral communication is thus the *Umma*. Muslims are part of this Umma, the "underground railroad," so to speak, of a global Islamic community allegiance. Muslims in London feel literally welded to and a cloned part of oppressed fellow Muslims in Palestine, for example. A rumor that the Quran was dishonored in one country caused a riot in Pakistan, an entirely different country. Can we as Christians not engage with worldwide Christians in the same way, in prayer, in support, and in partnership?

Practically speaking, why is the *Umma* community such a gift to westerners? Here is an example. Dressed in a black covering from head to foot, Suade seemed hospitable but imposing. My wife Evey went with Ashley, our 26-year-old ministry intern, to visit Suade, who pronounced the blessing of God as she entered her apartment. Suade then brought her husband, Chafic to our home. As we began telling the Prodigal Son story (Luke 15), Chafic took over and started to read the story himself. Then he became animated and began commenting on the story. "He insulted his father!" "He came back defiled. His father ran to see him?" "Why did his father do that?" I lost my job telling the story! The secret was to turn Chafic's hunger over to God rather than to make myself the one with all the answers. My Muslim friend showed that the Spirit of God was at work in his life. Later, Chafic invited us over to his home for a traditional Moroccan meal. Hospitality was Chafic's honorable way of saying that God was speaking to him and that he wanted to know more about God in the context of a meal together. God spoke. Hospitality was the response!

Muslims are part of a shame and honor culture vastly different from the Western guilt and consequence culture. Biblical teaching contains many themes on shame/honor as well as guilt/consequence themes: Jesus "endured the cross, scorning its shame" (Hebrews 12:2); "I honor my Father, and you dishonor Me" (John 8:49).

A Muslim who is shamed is a Muslim who feels defiled. Yet this concept of shame/honor is a gift to Western missionaries. What is often astonishing among Westerners is this: guilt in Islam must never be confessed, according to Muslim tradition, because it would result in a loss of honor which is worse than death itself. The Turks have a saying, "Even if guilt were made of silk, no one would wear it." An Arab proverb is, "Any injury done to a man's honor must be revenged, or else he becomes permanently dishonored."

Occasionally in ministry, I have felt like a plumber trying to do heart surgery because I did not have the proper knowledge to understand the principles of shame/honor. Zacchaeus climbed a tree (Luke 19) just to see Jesus. Jesus asked him to hurry down from the tree so he could eat at his house. Reverse hospitality? Yes, and more. Jesus honored this man who confessed his wrongdoing all the way home. (For those who spot every detail of Jesus' calling to Zacchaeus, note that the sycamore tree gave food for the poor, showing a tree of God's grace and abundance in a tree or lifeline genealogy of God's love and care.)

We normally describe grace as the unmerited favor that melts the sinner's heart. Among Easterners and Muslims, unmerited honor opens the door and melts the undeserving heart in the presence of the word of God, Jesus Christ. We often ask to eat or drink tea in a Muslim's home— and we ask it with urgency. They feel honored, which opens their heart and home.

Muslims have a concept of defilement that is not unbiblical. Ezekiel 22 records that "priests have done violence to my law, and have profaned my **holy** things; they have made no distinction between the **holy** and the **common**, neither have they caused men to discern between the unclean and the clean, and have hidden their eyes from my Sabbaths, and I am profaned among them." (emphasis mine; see also 1 Timothy 1:9, Hebrews 12:16) Biblical concepts of defilement are strange to a Western worker who may have relegated such teaching strictly to the Old Testament.

North African Muslims often place a car tire over their homes or carry the hand of Fatima or other talismans for protection against the *jinn*, or demonic powers. Being careful to eat with the right hand and to sleep on the right side, Muslims strive for a carefully balanced world.

Muslims need deliverance from anxiety about the defilement or shame that could befall them if they violate food or life codes. Freedom in Christ from defilement is another way of describing salvation. The concept of the *fitra* among Muslims is the quest for harmony in a world of chaos due to defilement. *Fitra* is the harmony of all things physical, submitting to what is spiritual and conforming to the orderliness of God. Yet disorder reigns for Muslims who will only find freedom from defilement in Christ.

When we focus primarily on grace and salvation from specific wrong acts, it is hard to have the needed compassion and sense of urgency for people trapped in murky defilement. My personal life in prayer before God has been radically transformed by the impact of honor and dishonor. No longer do I try to find sins to confess, though I would do this when necessary. Now I ask the Lord where I have dishonored Him and listen carefully for His instructions and strive to give God honor which is deserved by the Highest.

A better consideration for evangelization than what God requires or what points are needed for salvation is telling Muslims about Adam and Eve. Tell them that Adam and Eve were created without shame. They sinned and had to hide from their shame and defilement. Our Muslim background believer (MBB) church in Paris is led by an Algerian convert who came to Christ by reading the story of Adam and Eve in the garden. He saw that while Adam and Eve were defiled, God never left them. God called for the defiled couple, He clothed them, He corrected them, He gave a promise to them, and He kept them alive.

Muslims have never heard that God "associates with" or dialogues with and cherishes and even loves defiled people. In fact, the greatest form of blasphemy in Islam is the concept of *syirik*, or associating with impure people. For Muslims, relational involvement with people diminishes God's greatness. (God, they believe, never associates with humans because of an

extreme view of defilement.) But in Christ, the Samaritan woman (John 4) went from "worthless and defiled" to useful and valuable to God. In Christ, Onesimus, who was branded for life as useless, became useful and valuable to Philemon and to the Lord.

Our understanding of holiness and defilement is also a gift to us. We are learning to minister with compassion to people with defilement or addictions and codependency issues. Muslims do not feel that they are worthy or capable of being in a relationship with God due to their defilement. Jesus' carrying their sorrows and entering their darkness is more compelling to Muslims than logical steps or "to-do" lists.

If not "to-do lists, what do we say to people of other cultures?" Tell them a story, and tell them your story. The vast majority of the world's unreached are *oral peoples* (literate and non-literate), for whom the nature of communication is telling stories. For these people, storytelling is not only the way they communicate, but it is also the most effective way to spread the gospel. Oral people can usually recite back eighty percent or more of the stories they hear. By comparison, Western people can usually recite back twenty-five percent or less of what they hear.

Jesus used parables to communicate with the Jews, who were also oral people. The Parable of the Sower allowed the listener to become an active participant in the story. No parable can so demonstrate the call of the gospel to be freed from religion as the Parable of the Good Samaritan. Jesus loves to ease His disciples into cross-cultural or enculturation by speaking about the "half Jews," the good Samaritan, or the sinful Samaritan woman who was greatly loved by Jesus.

Each story is a mirror of the heart. A nomadic Tuareg pilgrim to Mecca came to me and asked for more and more stories from the Bible. He was trained in Quranic verses. I wondered how he would ever allow me to share openly with him in a

Western cultural form. Yet, as a storyteller, I was able to enter into his oral tradition world. He kept saying, "Don, tell me more stories from the Bible."

David, for example, noted the importance of always being ready to communicate stories. Psalm 45:1 reads, "My heart overflows with a goodly theme; I address my verses to the king; my tongue is like the pen of a ready writer." What does this mean to me? My tongue is always ready to communicate my heart and the heart of God, my king, whether through stories, laments, or songs.

Two significant treasures await the Western worker with this "gift of the story." First, we do not have to be experts in Islam to tell stories to Muslims. No need to tell them the fifteen things that they need to change to become a Christian. Instead, stories allow the teller to let the receiver hear and decipher without imposing the pressure of interpretation. Men's groups are best led by story-telling leaders than a number of bullet points in many nations. This is rarely admitted in Western cultures.

Second, by telling stories as Jesus did, we do not have to serve as the go-between for Muslims to constantly interpret God to them. We do not want to become a mediator between Muslims and God because we know that "there is one God and one mediator also between God and men, the man Christ Jesus" (1 Timothy 2:5). Becoming the mediator can run the risk of supplanting the role of Jesus. Also, we could become the "bookshelf of answers" that keeps the Muslim background believer from taking their questions directly to the word of God. Dependency is not the same as discipleship.

I continue to encourage the contextualization of our methods, our ministry, and our message to Muslims. My finding, however, is that the contextualization of the Western missionary is an acute need. Contextualized workers may not wear all the robes or know all the rites of their Muslim friends. Yet they are learners, having taken on the gifts of community, the gifts of shame and honor, the gifts of holiness and defilement, and the gifts of oral communication. I am taking a bottom-up approach that says, "Yes, I am Western, but Muslims can see that my Western heart is assimilating an Eastern worldview in light of God's word. Rather than a top-down, sophisticated, culturally-correct approach to the presentation of a contextualized gospel, let us get the word out that we need hundreds and thousands of unassuming workers with unstudied talent. We need Western and non-Western workers who are willing to be dramatically changed and strongly contextualized in their biblical thinking. The vast majority of the world's unreached are *oral peoples* (literate and non-literate), for whom the nature of communication is telling stories. Just talk. Just tell.

Chapter 5

Know the Story of My Friend Musa to See The Opposition and Strength of Faith

I grew up in Blida, Algeria—of parents who were suddenly lifted out of my life at the age of four. My father gave me to the Imam, saying Musa will be under your tutelage forever. To honor Islam, I became a Talibe boy, begging for all my food for money that went back to the Imam. I slept mostly in the sand with dozens of other Talibe boys. Harsh were the ways of the Imam, who beat every Talibe boy who had no money for the Imam's coffers. Blida, known as the City of Roses, taught me to love harshness and discipline in the Koran, recitations, and the discipline in the beatings that I began to welcome and love. My harsh treatment was all for Islam.

Years later, I was a known footballer, one of the best, going across northern Algeria with my team. Musa, Musa, Musa they shouted. We went up the Djurdjura Mountains in the Grand Kabylie where the Kabyle Berbers live. There we found a plateau where football teams like to practice. But the team found one member, Lehsan, suddenly sick with a bowel or appendix problem that made him writhe on the ground. He was clearly going to die.

We saw another team up there, hoping for a doctor for Lehsan. The other team was shockingly a team of perverted infidels called Christians. They wanted to pray for Lehsan. Little did I realize that this was to be the beginning of the infidel

Christian movement in Algeria, among college students who were sent out by an old praying woman in Algiers. We figured that prayer was like a talisman incantation, a powerful jinn or demonic power. So as they prayed, Lehsan was healed and stood up erect like a real sportsman. Sadly, the football team turned to the infidel Christian group and surrendered to this Isa-al-Masich, or Jesus, as they fell on their knees. I, too, went to my knees. But I never surrendered to Isa. I was the only one fully trained by the discipline of my Imam as a Talibe boy. Sure, I acted the part. But only I knew that this was a sick, disease-ridden way to try to become Western or Christian. I hated the cross and wouldn't bow to the cross.

Surely these Christians would be killed as they slaughter sheep once they leave this mountainous plateau. They ran into Mosque courtyards and shouted Isa, Isa, Isa, like my name was shouted so many times. Revenge came swiftly.

The decade of the '90s was so bloody that slaughter and destruction reigned supreme. The Afghan fighters, as they were called, were Algerians trained in Afghanistan by the Taliban. The message was clear. Islam needed to exert force and death, as the Koran says, Allah created first death and then life. Everything was purged, and government forces were decimated. Church buildings were forbidden, and Catholic White Fathers who remained in Algerian after the Franco-Algerian war were brutally killed. Roadblocks were death traps to all but the most disciplined Muslim Algerians.

To this day, after those torturous '90s, the Algerian soldiers and police have adopted the techniques of the Afghan fighters. The motto for any hostage situation is: first, protect the building or installation; second, kill all hostage takers; third, help the hostages if any are left. This was the modus operandi of the gas plant in southern Algeria when it was besieged. Many hostages were killed. But now, the soldiers are trained from the life and death of the Afghan fighters.

But during the 80s, my story begins. Harakat al-Shabaab al-Mujahideen (HSM) or al-Shabaab was principally a product of Al-Qaeda, but also at war with Al-Qaeda. Based mostly in Somalia, they extend with fingers into Africa. And I was called by a commander of al-Shabaab to meet him in Tizzi Ouzzu. (He knows my Imam from Blida, and then tracked me down.) He greeted me over a sandwich of egg omelet and fries: Hello, I am Sha! Assalam-o-Alaikum!

His greetings masked true intent. After praising my discipline in the book and in "the Religion," as he said, I expected my life to end immediately then and there. But no. Sha was very quick to put the cards on the greasy table. He said that Algeria needs me and fast. The reason was quirky and impossible to fulfill. I knew a blade awaited me if my answer was No. He said that the infidel Christians were crossing from the mainly backward Kabyle Berber group to other clans, Arabs, and even Egyptian Imams. So successful are these infidel Christian Berbers that the lamentable figure of 50,000 Christians in Algeria is told as a joke since the number is a multiple of that number.

What was I to do? Kill them all? I was baffled. No, I was to melt into the infidel Christian groups and discover why they are turning away from Islam. No argument, no anger, no defense of Islam, but to find out the secret of their massive expansion and to probe for any weakness that we could exploit. I said Yes. I'm now a member of al-Shabaab, an Arab Talibe boy, with the discipline of my Blida Imam, who called Sha to meet me. What was next?

Two Al-Shabaab Islamic Spies

Battle-hardened men on an espionage task in Algeria were educated and ready to die. Al-Shabaab, originally a Somalian Islamic terrorist group, is on the move. They are loosely connected with Al-Qaeda, the well-known group that has morphed into countries from Somalia to Mauritania. This book has never before unveiled the inner secrets of Al-Shabaab in Algeria. It is an espionage thriller of two very educated PhD Al-Shabaab scouts who are, at this very moment plotting the downfall of the country of Algeria, a nation rich in gas and petroleum. The observations are accurate and uncovered for the followers of the Holy Koran and of the Holy Bible.

Cigaal and Jimcaale became part of the espionage team after the significant setback at the gas plant explosion in southern Algeria. Cig and Jim are battlefield-hardened, using codes and loyalists to the cause of the Sharia-minded Salafists from

Saudi Arabia. To them, death is the open door to paradise—and they must not fail Allah with failed attempts. Word is already out that many Muslims in Algeria are following the Rasul Apostle Issa, otherwise known as Jesus.

Rather than facing the Infidel Christians directly, they want to discredit the whole movement. Jim and Cig move from Oran to In-Salah, to Constantine, and to Algiers. Motive? Their purpose is to expose the myths of the failed prophet of Allah called Issa or Jesus. This will be done after a clean and thorough scouring of tribes and ethnic groups that pretend to be Issa followers. The dual can switch from Algerian Arabic to Classical Arabic to any Berber language, as well as English and French, which they often use to pose as naïve tourists. They have killed before and will cut the throats of anyone who catches wind of their calling and duty. It is blamed on the Army of Algeria or the GIA Afghans, who were trained in Pakistan.

This year, Jimcaale, known as Jim, an explosives expert, burned down a church in In-Salah, while he seemed to be fearless. Their cache of the ordinance is disbursed all over Algeria by farmers with ox cart who have no idea what they are hiding or how dangerous C-4 and other forms of death they learned to handle in their Pakistan training camps. Remember that they are much more into espionage and gathering the nuances of Christian growth and fearlessness. Torture chambers are used to find out the truth of the motivation of followers of Issa and with whom these "Christians" associate.

We will begin our tour of Jim and Cig, and reveal what they call lies and deceptions from city to village. To further complicate their work, the thousands of churches in Algeria have hundreds of theologies due to the dictatorial style of church leadership, which may have only a couple of pages of the Bible and biblical opinion that is second and third-hand. Jim and Cig have both memorized the Koran and are masters at changing followers of Issa back to Islam. But I digress.

I, Musa, met Jim and Cig in a coffee bar in Tizzi Ouzzu and rapidly established a rapport with them. I didn't know how to approach them with the wonderful espresso coffee that I couldn't enjoy. They were as willing to interview me as I was to interview them. I knew I could go too fast and then be wiped out before nightfall. I, a tacit tourist, told them I was a committed Allah follower with Issa. Their French was better than their English, so we continued in French. I honored them for their hospitality and told them how I suffered in Cyprus with knife-wielding anti-Communist Muslims that thought I was a Communist. Also, my gratitude for being saved in the Sahara Desert by a Muslim when I was lost. I gave my blood to save a Muslim mother and baby who were hemorrhaging in a small oasis in the southern Sahara Desert. I guess I was too friendly to be executed summarily. God preserved my life as I honored these heartless Muslim spies. I agreed to meet later to read their findings. (In Arabic!!) That would be in a year. They kept their word, and we met in an undisclosed location because I knew their mission and accepted it, and they accepted me as weird but experienced. I had eaten their famous sandwich with an omelet and French fries—almost a symbol of really having been in Algeria among the poor.

Sha had a crucial plan for Jim. The two flew together to Somalia in a light plane to avoid any detection of their flight. Sha was older and never took care of himself, wearing underwear three days in a row and sleeping with hundreds of captured infidel slaves in Saana, Somalia. He smoked so many cigarettes a day that his teeth were yellowed and out of alignment. He suffered from lung disease, kidney problems, worms, heart disease, sexually transmitted diseases, and a horrible version of gangrene had caused his genitals to rot, turn black, and become infested with maggots—thus unable to sit on a chair, even in our airplane seat, without a toilet ring foam cushion. Sha was humanity almost as despicable as his hatred for the cross, the pig, and the filthy belief of the infidels. But Jim flew with this disease-ridden recruiter and strategist for "the Religion."

During the flight, I knew more than explosive techniques and wrote in my diary the destructive influence of Christians. This prepared me, I figured, to come back to Algeria and slip into the dark world of infidels and haram Christ followers that Allah assuredly wanted to be wasted from the earth.

Ask yourself what you will look like after reading this book. Most Christians are neither qualified to talk to Muslims about a loaf of bread, let alone spiritual matters. The same goes for this diary and this book. Why is this? It doesn't matter "why." You will indeed find the following to be aggressive in your face, and I give you permission to be angry. Christians are sloppy.

Some Muslims know the Bible better than Christians do. The Christian commitment to Isa-al-Masch is as deep as old hymns. Followers of Jesus sing 300-year-old songs and expect John Wesley to pop up old Christian songs. Isa followers may love Wesley hymns and love to sing them. But tell a Muslim, "Foul, I to the fountain fly," and their church nostalgia does not run deep and does nothing to 20-somethings or to us, the Muslims.

This diary is for people under 40. Unless you are in tune with the dynamic of the cultural dynamics of Rhianna, or at least the Bee Gees, you look backward. Is the Christian cultural dynamic big enough for what you are about to read? Would you agree that Jesus is a prophet? You better, or you've lost first base in baseball terms. If you are in your 60s like the author, and can dance with Muslims from Tizzi in Algeria and the young people who love Christian pop music, then you may not be as old-fashioned and irrelevant as I would expect some old-time missionaries to be. I, a Muslim, know more about followers of Jesus than most Christians.

Christian culture has to be broken open like an egg but exists like a closed-up castle. Does a bad accent from another culture offend you? Does the ethnic forcefulness of speech upset you? Are you surprised that Muslims despise Christians but are open to listening to following Jesus? You're busted if you talk on a couch to a Muslim with the Bible on the couch next to your thigh. If you are a chatty Kathy, forget it. "He who has an ear, let him hear." If you try to teach bullet points to a group of Muslims who are interested in Jesus, you may have lost the war and wasted their time and yours.

Don't you Christians know about the sin in your life? Mr. Christian, have you no shame? This non-starter gives Muslims shame over which they would prefer death. Guilt is so foreign that it comes from a Western construct that separates and dashes a Muslim's hopes of having a friendship with you. Go ahead and befriend a Muslim without sharing your belief system first, and you have just turned water into Kool-Aid. Christian, you are Kool-Aid drinkers. You watered down the Injil. It's like befriending a person and then selling them a used car the next day. So cheap. West must meet East.

Western Christians baptize after weeks of study. The Ethiopian was baptized right away. Handling an Easterner like a Westerner is like insulting a respectful people. Westerners cherish honesty or used to do so, and Muslims respect honor. It should cause a rise of frustration in you to promise a child a trip and then cancel it for the 20th time. You come with your answer in Jesus, and we Muslims are busy trying to balance a life of shame and dishonor. Don't promise the living God without addressing their greatest fear and thinking they are convinced of hell as the best deal they get. The best deal you will get out of this book is to break you open like an egg and restart your cross-cultural changes, even if changes in your life make you sad to have such a learning curve. A journey awaits you. Can you really take this crap, Christian? All I hear from Christians is crap. This is now the end of this portion of the diary since we are landing in Saana, where I'm hustled into a training center that can't be seen by drone attack planes. The landing is rough for Sha, who has to take morphine shots for his genital rot.

We observe the intensely trained Islamists and how they view Christianity. Can we be able to meet the onslaught of hatred and return the love of God in a way that honors the dishonorable who only know hate until someone like you uses oral discussion to reveal the love of Jesus in His parables, His healing, and in His caring for the dishonored since He cares for the poor and needy?

Chapter 6

Idolatry and Power from Dark Forces Are Meant to Hinder Cross-Cultural Outreach

I was in Algeria when I was called to hold a seminar for 200 of the most effective pastors among the Berbers in Tizzi Ouzzu, namely the Kabyles. They bought a cow for 200 pastors for the weeklong encouragement and teaching. We had a lot of rice and a bit of beef for dinner. It was clearly a cross-cultural seminar, taught fully in French. Before the seminar started, I asked a local pastor, a Kabyle, why most homes in the Greater Kabylia region have car tires on their rooftops. His answer was that tires protect the people inside from demons or jinn, since they believe that demons that attack the house will get caught up in the inner dimensions of the car tires and spin around and never enter the house.

Most astonishingly, I began to teach in French when the Spirit gave me a clear check in my heart to stop teaching but to ask all 200 key pastors a question. I asked them if any would have a power object or fetish (like a rabbit's foot) in their pocket to add protection to their life in Christ. I asked those who had power objects to stand. All 200 pastors stood up. I figured that I had miscommunicated the question. So after being seated, I asked them the same question. All 200 stood up. They were invited to put the power object on my Bible. All 200 came forward and covered my Bible with fetishes, shells, hands of Fatima, and more. The last object was a note addressed to me. "Pastor Don, forgive me, but I

36

have a flying carpet at home through which I travel from village to village. I will go home and burn it today."

How do you apply this in your cross-cultural context in your town or city? Simple. You don't have to suspect everyone who is Christian to carry a good luck charm in their pockets. This is a universal issue of possessing a house, a car, money, your profession, your spouse, or anything else that you turn to take the place of Christ alone or to find help outside or in addition to God's sovereign protection. No one needs to be a Pentecostal, Bapticostal, or Charismatic to know that we are to "have no other gods before the Father."

To find out information about spirits and the future and other matters of interest, many people use divination. These methods include astrology, reading the entrails of animals, using special stones, and astrology. This includes "*tarot* cards, palm reading, the *I Ching*, tea-leaf reading, observing how feathers fall, the throwing of cowrie shells, necromancy (contacting the dead) and interpreting dreams and visions. Note (Lev. 10.26), "Do not practice divination or sorcery," and see also (Deut.18:10). I don't even know my astrological monthly sign. Nor do I want to follow this demonic practice, which is announced on tv, radio, and on the internet. This is seeking information from demonic sources that are no cleaner than tires on Algerian rooftops.

Missionaries have been quite successful in reaching animistic people. In 1900, 9.2% of Africa was Christian. In 2000, 45.9% were. The population grew 626% in that period, while Christianity grew by 3,500%. Yet ethnoreligionists (tribal religions) were 117,537,000 in 1900 and 266,281,000 in 2009. In 1900, ethnoreligionists were 7.2% of the global population. In 2009, they were 3.9% of global population (World Christian Database). Their percentage is declining, while absolute numbers are increasing. I have often asked people who feel darkness in their lives, whether they had contact with Ouija boards, horoscopes, intimacy outside of marriage, rage or anger, unforgiveness, or even passivity in our Christian faith toward the last command of Jesus, to go to the nations and peoples with the gospel. We can reach out to non-Christians with any of the fivefold ministries mentioned in Ephesians: pastor, teacher, evangelist, church planter, or prophet. France, where I live, has Les Coupeurs de Feu, or extinguishers of fire. This is not the fire department, but dark-spirit-inspired people who live near every city in France. They do healing, cure physical pain, and intervene in sickness and disease through incantations. Shockingly, every pharmacy in France has the phone number and address of these dark-spirit healers, who are promoted and accepted as normal at every pharmacy in the country. Never think that darkness is only revealed in lesser developed nations. Keeping people free of darkness is allowing the so-called middle zone to be filled with Christ alone. The scandal of some politicians receiving millions of dollars to buy their vote and allegiance is a form of darkness that is as pernicious as any form of degradation before God since it betrays integrity and national trust.

In **Luke 8:27-40, we are shown the power of Jesus over the demoniac's torment.**

And when Jesus went around, He met a certain man outside the city, a man who had devils for a long time, and wore no clothes. Observe the parallel that exists between this poor demoniac and the unconverted sinner.

PREVIOUS TO CONVERSION

Jesus healed a man possessed by an unclean spirit, living among the dead, and disordered intellectually. He is his own tormentor, in a state of utter destitution and wretchedness, beyond the power of human assistance or restraint.

AT CONVERSION

The means employed was the Word of Christ. The influence exerted was the almighty power of Christ. The effect produced the following: The unclean spirit was expelled. The naked one was clothed. The wanderer sat at the feet of Jesus. The maniac was now in his right mind.

AFTER CONVERSION

Desiring to remain with Jesus, how natural it was, wishing to forsake all in order to be near the Great Physician. Christ's command, whatever it may be, was immediately obeyed.

Chapter 7

Honor, Adultery, Radio DVDs, and a Dancing Christian

Musa told me more about His journey. My training was not a set of charts and Power Points. In Yemen, training required me to slaughter sheep with a knife to the throat in the Halal (acceptable to Allah) way and to do the same to captured prisoners. I watched the imprisoned women become selected for the sexual pleasure of the ISIS and Al-Shabaab fighters finish their daily training with delight in the women of their choice. The Koran in Sura 4:24 says: *And forbidden to you are wedded wives of other people except those who have fallen in your hands (as prisoners of war).* All the men jumped into hot bathtubs afterward to atone for their possible dishonor to Allah. Once totally submerged, all misdeeds were purified and Halal to Allah. (A woman who commits adultery, in Islamic requirements, must take a bath to restore her purity. There is no accountability to God or a search for forgiveness from the Lord.)

During my training time, the Sha died and was buried the same day. We knew he would have 72 virgins to engage in blissfulness before Allah after his swift burial. Before his death, he conferred on me his approval for the mission of entering Algeria to discover why the filthy infidels are becoming cross-bearing and filthy Christians. I was rushed to Algiers by night, and I headed directly for Oran, west of Algiers. I met Cigaal briefly in Algiers, where he remained as my logistics manager and record keeper.

Traveling to Ain Temouchent, south of Oran, I met a Christian known for his stupid ignorance but Christian life in a radius of 200 km. His church was vibrant and loud in the hot, baking sun. Pastor Rachid was ready to talk to me after his Friday church meeting. Why are you a filthy infidel Christian, I asked. Who are these people that were Muslim and now following the Isa-al-Maschich (The Messiah)? He explained that in Algeria, no church is permitted without first having a building. No sharing of the infidel message of Jesus is permitted outside of that building.

Pastor Rachid was different from my Talibe days in Blida, where we had to beg for food and give all our money to the Imam under his strong and whipping arm. Rachid said that he is not a Jew, not an American, not a Frenchman, but an Arab Algerian. But Rachid said, "Christianity is from the West, not from us." Not stopping to argue, Rachid explained that he had a withered leg, his left leg. When his wife told Rachid she was carrying his 7th baby, he immediately reached for an old revolver, something left over from the French Revolutionary War. Rachid was shamed. He knew Western Christians would never understand that death is better than being shamed and dishonored. Western Christianity is water thin, I used to think.

Rachid was a stupid farmer with one useless leg that he pulled along. Now having an extra mouth to feed, the dishonor was more than he would live with. We are now off to the coffee bar in Oran. He ordered a coffee espresso with his pistol on the table. Ready to drink and shoot his brains out, Rachid was to end it then and there. But the coffee bar had a visitor who looked like a salesman. He gave a booklet to Rachid called the Injil/Gospel of Luke. The booklet stuck to the filthy table like spilled food never met a cleaning rag. Out walked the salesman. Luke was a doctor who knew Jesus, Isa, thousands of years ago. Rachid read two pages and fell to the ground under some unexplained power. This happened twice. Hobbling home almost like someone with a stroke, Rachid was greeted by his wife with ululating, the tongue flipping over the half-closed mouth. Rachid found a niche behind the barn and read the Luke Injil cover to cover. He kept falling down under the power—whether by Allah's power or Satan's power, he didn't know.

Jim said to Rachid, "Well, so what? So what? My dishonor was lifted off me like a flax sheet. Without dishonor, I gave my future and all my family to Jesus, Isa-al-Maschich. He lifted me up, and I became a Christian. Jim again, And so what? You are a Muslim, born a Muslim, still a mixed-up Muslim."

Dear Cigaal,

As we started our journey, we met this infidel, Priest Rachid. He gathered Christians who no longer follow the hajj (pilgrimage journey to Mecca) or the Blessed Koran or Mohammed, blessed be his name. Rachid carries a cross around his neck because he fell down under the power of the demonic jinn. This was filth in the name of Allah. He doesn't know the curse of the hand of Fatima or the death that awaits him because he made a deal with the devil. His offspring will be mute, maimed, and deranged. Falling down under a curse made Rachid, the priest think that he could break the families of people 200 km around his stinking church warehouse. He talks about Isa, Jesus, but never talks about the jinn that besots his world with a cloud of darkness. These Christians are multiplying like rabbits, but the dumb followers of Jesus are probably half as educated but devoted to pulling out fellow ummah Muslims and bringing the fitra order of Islam into mass darkness.

The best example is my next strategic discovery trip. Traveling east to El Marsa, I ate some kebabs and couscous (they say Moroccan couscous is better). I was worn out by the eerie feeling I had with this last priest, who I call the falling priest. After spending the night in a cheap hotel in El Marsa, I opened the shutters in the morning only to survey the lay of the land. However, my view was a rusting junk yard of old cars and metal parts for about 100 meters. The hotel owner was especially nice to me by giving me two blankets that had been washed one time in never. The mattress was surely from the 1800s—don't laugh—broken springs and all. I heard the prayer call and did my Salat prayers toward Mecca, scaring off Satan and invoking Allah as having one prophet, Mohammed. The hotel rug even had a compass built into the rug to aim straight to Mecca.

On the road, I went hunting for a totally ignorant shepherd, Asan, who was 120 km south of El Marsa. Taxis are cheap, and busses stop at everyone's house, taking you through the chickens and goats and human stench in a place where it never rains. I found him. Asan, the shepherd, had a reputation that is known for hundreds of kilometers around his sheepfold, where he raised up another cursed church.

He greeted me and ran to give me water from his well and figs and olives, dates, and even instant coffee. We talked. He knew I never was a Muslim; also, that I was sent out to set up for the kill by Al-Shabaab. (I have to take care when visiting a Christian. Either Christians will pollute me with the demonic jinn and their blue eyes—or if the police come for any pretext, they have a new way of operating. They learned this in the 1990s and carried it out during the attack on the gas plant not far from the southern town of Tamanrasset.)

Following the bloody days of the 1990s in Algeria, the so-called Afghans, Algerians trained in Afghanistan, taught a frightening example to the police. Priorities first: First, secure the gas plant; next, kill all assault agents; and lastly, help the hostages if there are any left. No one negotiates with hostages in hand in Algeria. All die. Story over.

The Pickup Truck Story and Playing a DVD on a Radio

Asan was another Priest who calls himself Pastor Asan. He told the story of his recent life. Two Christians were on the road from El Marsa in a

44

truck filled with video DVDs of this prophet Jesus or Isa to give to everyone in the El Marsa area and on the farm roads to the south. The pickup truck in front of them was running over rough roads. A suitcase bounced out of the pickup truck. So the two Christians sped up and tried to pass the pickup truck to warn the pickup chauffeur. Not a chance. The pickup sped up, fearing roadside bandits in the Christian truck. So both trucks sped up. Finally, both trucks stopped, figuring maybe it was the will of Allah. The two Christians implored the pickup driver to go back to pick up the airborne suitcase. "No, not unless you come with me, because I'm afraid to go back on my own." The Christians said, "Forget it. It is only one kilometer back, and it is your suitcase, so go get it."

The two Christians drove on a short distance and ran over a sheep and killed it. Desperately distraught, the Christians went to the shepherd and offered to pay for the loss. No, he said, since it hasn't been dead for long, its soul is still in it, and we can have it for couscous. They stayed and ate the roadkill. But the lamb was the pet of shepherd Asan's two children who were crying. Out of the need to offer a hospitality gift, the two Christians offered Asan a DVD. Just imagine how classic this was for a poor farmer and rancher. The shepherd Asan said, "I don't even have a radio to play it on." See how stupid these people are? Dumb as a sack of hammers.

But then Asan's neighbor was watching a television broadcast from France. Through this, the neighbor became a traitor to our cause and called Jesus more than a prophet, blasphemously, the Son of God. The neighbor brought over a player for the shepherd's DVD, and the kids watched until they nearly wore it out. Asan is now a follower of Isa, as is his church people, and so are the people who drive in by cars and taxis and busses to come for Friday meetings that last all day.

Dear Cigaal,

Dumb as hammers, this Christian shepherd didn't demand payback for a lamb that was run over. He thought that DVDs played on radios. By watching a plastic DVD dozens of times, shepherd Asan changed from being part of our ummah fellowship to turning his back on the Religion. He thinks Allah caused the killing of the lamb. He cooked a meal with the repulsive infidels and fed them with the roadkill. I wanted to say this Asan will snap out of it in a few months when Ramadan comes and Muslim neighbors come to his house. They may stone him for this treachery. People come from all over, and they follow his story, and now they have watched the DVD and memorized each word of Jesus. They leave out of this shepherd's sheepfold and go in all directions with memorized words of Jesus that heal people as they hear the words. This DVD plastic disk is maybe the reason infidels are changing the face of Asan's sheepfold. But two hundred people is not our worry. This is a story of kids that liked that plastic disk. We need to see kids trained in the Talibe way and learn the discipline I had with my Imam. I'm telling you, Cigaal, kids in Algeria need Talibe discipline to stop the spread of this brand of infidels. Send this info back to the base with the other letter. And hurry.

The Dancer

I made a trip further to the east from El Marsa to follow the A1 highway near the Kabyle area of Algeria to the church founded by the Dancer in El Harrouch. Rosa and her husband were married for two years, during which time Rosa remained a Muslim, though her husband was an infidel, a Christian. Rosa and Mohammed lived for two years, with Rosa reciting the "bismallah" perhaps a dozen times a day in oaths, arguments, and occasions where truth needs to be verified. During the purification for Rosa's salat prayers, the bismallah recited, "In the Name of God, the Merciful, the Compassionate." The bismallah is repeated in full during the rak'as parts of prayer, immediately after a confession of the need for protection from the "Cursed One," or Satan. Protection from the "Cursed One" is as the auzobillah: "I seek refuge in Allah from the Cursed One." It is "In the name of Allah, the Merciful and Compassionate One. Praise belongs to Allah, the Lord of the worlds, the Merciful Compassionate One. Guide us into the straight way, the way of those on whom Thou hast bestowed favor, not of those against whom there is anger, nor of those going astray." Mohammed listened to this a dozen times a day from Rosa. Rosa was attempting to control the powers of fate and misfortune in life with the curses and interfaces with the salat prayer rituals. whether benign or malevolent, forces occupy a place of harmony within the framework of Muslim thinking.

But Mohammed had another idea, and it ended in a church that was planted with Mohammed and Rosa the dancer. How did this happen? Rosa was cursing herself by reciting the bismallah, though we Muslims want the void filled, whether by curses or by good spirits. "Like, Allah, just fills the void with good or evil spirits, but just do it."

Rosa had a bigger curse on her life if she became a Christian since she would have dishonored her father and family. So, brave and stupid, Rosa went to her father's house and asked her father, "Should I become a Christian or should I divorce my husband, Mohammed?" Her father walked out, angered, with nothing to respond to in any suitable way. He was mad as hell.

So Rosa, the woman wearing a double curse, the bismallah curse, and the family curse looming on her life, decided to go to bed in her childhood bedroom. I had to know how it came out from this doubly cursed woman of spiritual bastardness. Rosa, what happened?

"I, Rosa, went to bed, and spirits came under my bedroom door and lit up like a thousand candles, and they talked to me with these words: 'What do you want me to do for you tonight?' I ran downstairs and cried to my mother since my father wouldn't talk to me. Mother said, 'Oh, Rosa, we have jinn demon powers in our house all day and all night. They move our furniture, move our pictures on the wall, and leave filth in the toilet. Just drink a half glass of water, and they will go away.' The next night I had the same thousand candles talking to me and asking the same question. I drank half a glass of water, and they went away. The third night, prepared for the demons, readied with half a glass of water, the spirits asked me what they should do for me. Somehow, I knew that somewhere in this light was the Father of Lights, my husband Mohammed's God, asking what He could do, whereas my father was pouting and powerless. More, just at this miraculous moment, Mohammed knocked on the door. Mohammed asked, 'Rosa, please come home with us, your family.' Rosa said, 'I will be your wife, and Jesus/Isa will be my Lord.'"

That was enough for me. Her daughter had crushing headaches. Rosa told her daughter Fatima to be free in Jesus' name. Fatima was free. Now this Dancer in El Harrouch, in their ACCM Church, is drawing people who dance in the Kabyle fashion as they hear the reading of the Bible.

Dear Cigaal,

This Rosa thinks that she can dance her way out of the ummah of Islam. Allah will never speak to her, just like her father. She is so filled with curses and spirits that will ruin her life. More than ever, husbands of Islam have to insist that their wives not curse their families by leaving Islam. The dishonor of the father needs the village to bring vengeance upon the offender, Rosa, in this case— her body burned or her life shunned by the whole town. Even a young woman who spurns the advances of a Muslim young man will tell the father, who will assign the older son to cause great harm to the young lady who has dishonored the family by saying no. This is going to stop these churches dead in their tracks by bringing vengeance against the sickening dishonor of the family. We have a church, the ACCM Church, full of dishonored people. Also, dishonoring Allah, they will be held in the hell of fire by Allah, to whom dishonoring Allah is not tolerated. Bismillah will return to curse this woman Rosa and her husband Mohammed. Send this to the base. Honor is at stake, and honor is not going to be an option.

Chapter 8

Cross-Cultural, Encultured Life and Intercultural Meetings May Focus on Wounded and Despised People

I'm tired and catatonic from the encounters I've had. My energy level is high, and I'm going to change strategies from church interviews to something more telling. Are these followers of Jesus just talkers, or do they really help the nation of Algeria? Anyone can talk, but who cares for earthquake victims, mudslides, and our lack of water? Where are the followers of Isa? This is a radical change for me to change my pace.

According to the religion of Mohammed, they say the following: "True, our Religion of Peace says in the Koran, Qur'an (4:34) Men are the maintainers of women because Allah has made some of them to excel others and because they spend out of their property; the good women are therefore obedient, guarding the unseen as Allah has guarded; and (as to) those on whose part you fear desertion, admonish them, and leave them alone in the sleeping-places and beat them; then if they obey you, do not seek a way against them; surely Allah is High, Great."

First of all, I visited a female Marabout (a fortune teller), Rania, who made a small fortune in foretelling the future. She would welcome a customer and listen to the jinn/demons, and pronounce the evil they had planned for the clients. It was a perfect set-up until one day, Rania felt she was deceiving her friends, neighbors, and

51

others. This was all happening in Setif, part of Kabylia, which the locals call Tamurt. Rania refused to listen to the jinn and pronounce their demonic and degrading ways. This cost her money and physical bruises all over her body, a curious case of demons causing physical harm. We think that demons are in a spiritual world and can't hurt us physically. Think again.

Second, Rania's husband heard of this and was dishonored. He beat up his wife and divorced her. A divorced woman in Algeria, to be honest, is like a leper, treated less than a dog. She ran to the White Fathers to find an answer to her degradation, still being a Muslim. She spoke to a French priest named by the Bishop of Algiers as Christian Cheissel, 36 years old. (The White Fathers were committed Christian Catholics who were all martyred in Algeria.) He directed Rania to the followers of Isa who loved her into Isa's family or ummah. I contacted Rania, who is now busy translating parts of the Kabyle Bible from the French Bible.

Sure, she was called a perverted reprobate Muslim, dishonoring her husband and Allah as well. She was rejecting the jinn/demon voices that were sent directly from Allah, the idolatrous and demonic so-called god. Rania was pretty much a degraded example of Muslim existence. She left the ummah/fellowship and the Religion. Hell awaits her, they said. But as I asked around, I found the Center for the Rehabilitation of Muslim Women in Constantine. It was led by Nesrine, a Pakistani Muslim. She has 50 beds for women who have been beaten for divorcing their husbands and others for dishonoring or disobeying their husbands. I was able to ask Nesrine for more information about these women who obviously defiled Islam. "Nesrine, why don't these women leave their homes as soon as they are beaten for the first time? What happens after three months of your care of these women?"

Not many men are allowed in here. But outside this complex, I guess it's safe and honorable. Many, many women of Islam, not all, but most feel that beatings are part of their lot and place in life as married women. They expect it and look forward to it daily to satisfy Allah, until they collapse and are thrown out of the house. After three months of care, they all get **jobs** for food and clothing. It is always prostitution. There is no one else who will employ a debased woman here.

"But Don, I'm closing this center in a month for good." The reason is that so many women are victims of acid thrown in their faces that we have to fill the center with these women first. Completely disfigured, they have lost even the smallest drop of self-esteem. All will leave after three months and go into prostitution, covering their faces to hide from their customers. We have a waiting list that far eclipses the capacity of this complex. Men think that acid will keep them from ever finding another man. They were damaged for life. "I analyzed that Allah had a purpose and that it was his will for these women. After all, a woman has the importance of only half a man. Men rule here in Islam, of course."

This doesn't tell me the answer of the followers of Isa toward beaten or acid women. But they have a life extension of 3 months with me at the Center. I didn't feel sadness or feelings of remorse over this situation. It just reinforced my conviction that women were made for pleasure, not to cause pain to their husbands. Of course, this is why older men seek to marry much younger women. They are obedient, like a daughter to a father. The children, in any case, belong to the father because they are his.

So what are the followers of Isa (Jesus, concerning us) going to do with this? Just preach and teach? Just talk about the prophet who could never replace the last prophet, Mohammed? This is the subject of my search. I am sure that my search will reveal their true colors of avoidance and play their merry games of singing their introverted music and dancing to the repulsive sounds of guitars and further shame

Allah and the Religion.

I found Sara in Constantine after landing at the Mohamed Boudiaf airport. I traveled just north of Constantine to Didouche Mourad, a small town nearby. Sara was a follower of Isa, well acquainted with acid and beating victims among Algerian women. She startled me by quoting the Bible almost immediately, "Husbands, love your wives, as Christ loved the church and gave himself up for her. And Psalm 150 (Psalms is called the Zabur) is the climax of the climax, where we are exhorted 13 times .... If you love the Lord (and honor your wife), you're going to get excited about gathering with His people to praise His name.

I was growing impatient with Sara, giving me more Bible and less evidence of help or solutions for battered women. "Don, you're right, we don't have a center with beds as they have at Nesrine's complex. We don't need this. We gather groups of 3 or 4 to share and cry after renouncing the flood that has permitted this abuse. Don, the flood is, so sorry to say, the Koran, which permits wife beating. The first stage is to collapse into the loving arms of Isa (Jesus) and become a follower of Isa. Islam, according to our first stage, has to be uprooted."

Sara, how does changing from the Religion not further defile the women who brought this down upon themselves? "Don, women of Islam are looking at beatings as a part of their lot in life. Who can support this degraded view of women? A loved wife is a better wife for you too, Don. "Our second phase is prayer in the power of the spirit of Allah, to restore and renew these women who are like babies, without willpower, wilted down and emptied of value and worth. Then we take them, one or two at a time, into our homes, treating them as part of our family fellowship or ummah.

"The third phase is a celebration, only if they are ready. They go to conferences where abused women listen to other women who have been set into a renewed lifestyle. They wear their traditional dresses and dance together and cry, cry, and cry. The memories are there, but they become even outspoken for other women who find themselves trapped and unable to find freedom outside of Isa." Sara, do they get jobs? "Don, jobs are for industrious and high self-worth individuals. They are creating a new Algeria, certainly locally. Don, this is not your Algeria."

Jim and Cig wrote about their view of the danger they thought of the rehab centers for women. "My mind is in a vice. I've been touring centers of rehabilitation for abused women. Somehow, I, as a man, had been given permission to talk to the leaders of an Islamic rehab center, led by Nesrine, and then by Sara, a follower of Isa. It seems to all boil down to how you view women. I think that women can soon be taking over a man's role and dominate our very Islamic Religion and society. Women are already in the military and work hard with Al-Shabab, strong and tough. Our society doesn't reflect the military's use of women. I really don't want to care, in my heart of hearts, whether women are abused or beaten since I've been brought up with this thinking. Even in the Arabian Kingdom, women can't drive cars and have no possession of the children. Remember Rania and her refusal to obey the jinn/demons sent from Allah. How can someone in disobedience to Allah ever have a place in society? Tell headquarters that the followers of Isa want to restore women as outspoken mouthpieces of rebellion. Degradation and defilement must fall on them, surely."

Paul Interacted Cross-Culturally with the Men of Athens by Understanding Their Culture

Paul was "audience-sensitive without being audience-driven" because he had the right attitude toward culture, namely, affirming as well as confronting culture. Because of these attitudes, Paul was able to be "a Jew to the Jews and as a Greek to the Greeks" (1 Cor 9:19-23). Paul's 'at-homeness' within overlapping Jewish, Greek, and Roman environments put him in a singular position to contextualize the gospel for both Jews and Gentiles, not as a foreigner, but as a cultural insider." Paul's Areopagus speech to the Athenians (Acts 17:22-34) clearly demonstrates his cultural sensitivity and "at-homeness" with his audience and therefore serves as a compelling example of ideal cross-cultural exchange. While this comes from the book of Acts, Luke nevertheless depicts a genuine character of the historical Paul. In this missionary sermon, Paul demonstrates a willingness to interact with the worldview, beliefs, and practices of his audience. He began the speech by saying, "You Athenians, I see that in every respect you are very religious. For as I walked around looking carefully at your shrines, I even discovered an altar inscribed, 'To an Unknown God'" (17:22b-23).

Paul is fully aware of the Athenian culture, religious beliefs, and practices. He also shows a remarkable familiarity with the Athenian's philosophical traditions by quoting well-known sayings from their philosophers and poets. Paul uses this insight to respectfully engage their worldview, drawing upon indigenous language, images, and concepts to communicate the gospel in culturally relevant forms. While Paul takes a respectful and conciliatory approach by beginning where the audience is, Paul does not simply conform to their worldview and beliefs, but rather he seeks also to confront and to correct and transform their understanding of God.

Isaac Watts, in 1719 didn't write this to initially be a Christmas carol, as the lyrics do not reflect the Virgin birth of Jesus, but rather Christ's Second Coming. An interlude that depends more on Watts' interpretation of the Psalm 98 text, stanza three speaks of Christ's blessings extending victoriously over the realm of sin. The cheerful repetition of the non-psalm phrase "far as the curse is found" has caused this stanza to be omitted from some hymnals. But the line makes joyful sense when understood from the New Testament eyes through which Watts interprets the Psalm. Stanza four celebrates Christ's rule over the nations. The nations are called to celebrate because God's faithfulness to the house of Israel has brought salvation to the world.

1.   Joy to the world, the Lord is come!
Let earth receive her King;
Let every heart prepare Him room,
And heav'n and nature sing,
And heav'n and nature sing,
And heav'n, and heav'n, and nature sing.
2.   Joy to the earth, the Savior reigns!
Let men their songs employ;
While fields and floods, rocks, hills, and plains
Repeat the sounding joy,

Repeat the sounding joy,
Repeat, repeat, the sounding joy.
3.   No more let sins and sorrows grow,
Nor thorns infest the ground;
He comes to make His blessings flow
Far as the curse is found,
Far as the curse is found,
Far as, far as the curse is found.
4.   He rules the world with truth and grace,
And makes the nations prove
The glories of His righteousness,
And wonders of His love,
And wonders of His love,
And wonders, wonders, of His love.

Chapter 9

Unexpected Cross-Cultural Results

Most of us know the story of Balaam and Balak, king of the Moab, who asked the wicked prophet Balaam to curse the Israelites because they were too powerful. Balaam was commissioned to ask God to curse the Israelites. Balaam sought the Lord four times to ask the Lord to curse Israel (Numbers 22). Famously and unforgettably, the Lord said in Numbers 23:20, "Behold, I have received commandment to bless: and he has blessed, and I cannot reverse it."

Balaam came up with a brilliant but shameful idea. He could not persuade the Lord to curse the Israelites, New Testament verses show that Balaam's plan was to have King Balaak send pagan women to swarm into the camps of the Israelites and to draw the Israelites into idolatry. Now the Lord who would not curse the Israelites was forced to bring judgment and a curse upon God's own people. This was an unexpected result in the Moabites bringing a cross-cultural defeat upon God's own people.

No place is cross-cultural madness seen than in the book of Jonah. God sent Jonah to Nineveh to proclaim certain doom upon the Ninevites without any promise given to the Ninevites for a way to change the judgment of God as definite and promised. But Jonah would not accept cross-cultural preaching from his Jewish background to the evil and pagan Ninevites from Assyria. It was a message to all of Israel that they were called to proclaim the God of Israel to the nations to fulfill the covenant of God to all the nations written in Genesis 12 and spoken to Abraham. We know of Jonah's ship not toward Nineveh but to Tarshish. Tarshish had the meaning of "breaking, beaten down, and shattered." Nineveh, the capital of Assyria, the world's first super power, had the meaning of handsome and agreeable. Jonah was swallowed by a fish as he cried out to God for three days inside that aquatic monster. Jonah, the unwilling cross-cultural prophet and preacher, finally preached certain doom to Nineveh. The people of Nineveh all repented and put on sackcloth, came to call upon God, even to Jonah's great displeasure of "loss of face" over the Lord's relenting on His promise to destroy the city. The Lord changed His mind based on His mercy, which was more His desire than to honor His word of promised destruction. We should never have a sour face if some wicked person comes to Christ. Remember Jesus' story of the last worker receiving the same wage as the first worker. Is that fair? Yes, because mercy triumphs over judgment.

The wise men, actually astrologers, were mercifully drawn to Bethlehem to see the Savior born to Mary. Did they make a mistake in announcing a king would be born as they spoke to jealous King Harrod, who subsequently murdered all children, baby boys, and toddlers under two years of age? Thousands were murdered. Admittedly, the weeping of mothers at the birth of Jesus was predicted and prophesied in the Old Testament. However, Nineveh was predicted by the Lord God to be totally destroyed because of their evil and demonic worship. After Jonah finally preached total destruction, devastation, and darkness to Nineveh, God changed his deadly promise for that city and placed mercy over the fulfillment of His own word. Could God have overturned the prophecy in the Old Testament of mothers weeping for their babies being murdered? Mercy is always preferred over judgment. Could the Maggi, or should the Maggi have not mentioned Jesus as a rival king? The Maggi were in the vortex of spiritual warfare with darkness and life. This should give us hope that where doctors or other people may proclaim rejection to our lives, God can invoke mercy over judgment in our lives and in the most difficult cross-cultural ministries to ethnic peoples who have gone far from God. Don't give up. Pray more and pray still more. God answers prayer against all odds.

There is also the potential in cross-cultural ministry for failure, which we have known many times. I tried to plant a church among the French to find that one member of the congregation arrived one hour late during my preaching. The whole church stopped, regardless of being in the middle of a message, and stood up and did the double cheek kiss to this member and late arriver. That was not very shocking, but a little shocking. Then she walked up to the platform and went to the communion bread and wine, and helped herself to the communion elements. We had already served communion. But we had to let her have communion since she came from a Catholic background and felt that she would go to hell if she missed a Sunday communion. I then understood why she ate the bread and drank the wine in such an ill-timed and provocative manner. I was truly shocked but I never stopped trying to plant a church among the French. I was more successful in assisting in the planting of a Sri Lankan, Tamil-speaking church and assisting a Haitian church, and finally, the successful planting of the first Muslim-convert or MBB (Muslim Background Believer) church in France.

No one has the silver bullet for a "successful" cross-cultural ministry. But we must reach out and try to follow the command of the Lord, "and behold, I will be with you always, to the end of the ages."

Chapter 10

Prayer, Essential and Fruitful in Encultured Outreach

For effective cross-cultural ministry, we must train new and old Christians to pray, not teach them, but to pray with them, knowing that praying even for a Muslim at a meal, they make a strong issue of not allowing us to pray in the name of the Father, the Son, and the Mother, their concept of the Trinity. Pray for Muslims on the street or another nationality on the streets. Pray for Assimah and her homework. Ask them to pray for Don, me. Ask another person to pray for Don to know Jesus better. Make them the cross-cultural king or queen.

Pray for the needs of a person of another culture, and thus get to know their needs and your care for them and the results of God's intervention in Christ. Ask for knowledge of their pain and suffering so you can pray and see Christ's healing power. Ask to pray for their sorrow. Pray for their spiritual leader, their Imam or Sheik or Mary Mother figure or statues they worship, regardless of how evil. Walk in 2s or 3s Sense spiritual darkness, and pray for their spiritual leaders by name. Pray for a person of peace, a person recognized with influence in the community. When Muslims or other ethnic groups find out that we are praying for them, they flood with joy.

Don't be bound by men only talking to men and women only talking to women. In Uzbekistan, seven churches were planted by women, making seven totally women-initiated churches. From

Acts 16:14, "Now a certain woman named Lydia heard us. She was a seller of purple in the city of Thyatira, who worshiped God. The Lord God opened her heart to heed the things spoken of by Paul." Honor another culture but don't be a slave to the new culture.

We know of several Christian ministry workers who so accepted the Muslims in their culture that they gave themselves over to becoming Muslims and even denying their faith in Christ. Entire mosques are becoming filled with followers of Jesus. The Muslims now bring their Bibles to the mosques and listen to the Imam share the Gospel of Christ. This enculturation is at a high level. Let's believe God for miraculous levels of God's intervention cross-culturally via great prayer in power and urgency.

Most cross-cultural movements among Muslims, Hindus, or Hispanics begin with prayer. One discipled and converted Muslim said, "There is no way you are going to succeed in ministry to ethnic or cross-cultural peoples coming to Christ if you don't succeed in believing in the power of prayer if you don't practice what prayer is.

Note that other cultures may speak to you sometimes 2 inches away from your face. Don't be alarmed, but offer to pray for your cross-culture fellow traveler that you may enter their home to break off any demonic influences, or dark influences, in the name of Jesus. Ask Jesus in prayer right then and there to give you the power to speak out deliverance so that the person can be free as they open their hearts to Jesus and willingly first confess Jesus Christ as Lord. That is a daring and wonderful prayer that comes with the joy of being a mature Christian in love with Jesus.

Ask for prayer teams to back you in prayer, to join you in prayer, and to bring down the full power of God that goes beyond setting up great programs and winsome ideas to draw people to church who need prayer and need to reach out in prayer in Jesus' name. That is action.

Chapter 11

Offended Muslims Laugh at a Personal God: Now Followers of Jesus Imagine that Allah Speaks

Cig, these followers of Isa (Jesus) have a tenacity that only a knife to the throat can remedy. I know we are not to engage in mass killings, but the Harakat al-Shabaab al-Mujahideen (HSM) or Al-Shabaab leaders want to pinpoint these followers of Isa. Since I could not locate all or even a small part of these defilers of Islam, I may be called back to Somalia and face a grilling or worse. They may have me sow Muslims into the gathered groups who report on the followers of Isa. I have to travel across Algeria to meet a Chaoui follower to hear about this notion that Allah speaks, which apparently attracts many hundreds of followers. It sounds like an insult to Allah, a dishonor to the Religion, and defecation upon the grave of Mohammed. I'm sickened even thinking of this trip.

They call themselves, Chaoui and number 5 to 7 million people. They are used in the police and army in Algeria since they are mostly mindless and unyielding to mental processes. This will prepare my trip in the future to Tamanrasset, the garrison city in the south that is guarded by Chaoui soldiers. These Berbers are called the Chaoui people. They live in eastern Algerian near and among the Aures Mountains, a refuge against the swarms of Arabs who came from Egypt on a crusade to convert North Africa by the sword. So I leave tomorrow for Batna, a town in Chaoui land. This speaking Allah pastor will wait for me at 3 pm in Batna at his church. Pastor Hocine was there to meet me at his church in Batna. I figured that this weird freak of an Isa follower was somehow filled with the jinn/demons and probably as dangerous as they come. But he was kind enough to offer me mint tea, dates, and olives as we sat down. After a short greeting, I introduced myself as Jim, also very interested in Isa/Jesus. Allah would forgive my lying lips, and so would al-Shabaab, his probable executioners in weeks or months ahead for lying and pretending to be interested in Jesus.

Hocine, "You are a pastor and one who has a group of 200 people attending your church. I heard you talk about Allah speaking, and I want to hear why you tell this to your people." Hocine replied that his fellowship has 300 people now and is outgrowing his building. He said that all his people hear the speaking Allah.

I got angered at this point and seethed with revulsion. I reminded Hocine that the Koran says that Allah will not associate with human beings but instead sends us blessings and curses, the jinn (demons), and opens the way to heaven if we walk along the small thread to paradise after we die. The Holy Koran says, "Allah does not forgive us if we are partners with Him; but He forgives anything else, to whom He pleases; to set up partners with Allah is to devise a sin most heinous indeed." --Sura 4:48. So Allah does not associate or speak with human beings, since they would then become unforgiven partners, and never forgiven for speaking with Allah.

Hocine said, Jim, you have darkness as your counselor, and you follow a dead teaching that makes Allah your silent enemy. Jim, let me explain. One of the Holy books is the Holy Bible, which Allah would never permit to be corrupted. So don't even think of the Holy Bible as corrupted unless your view of Allah is too weak to prevent the corruption of His Word. Jim, someone gave me a Holy Bible, and I began to read it, all about the Garden of Eden, Adam and Eve, and the sin that entered the world. It wasn't long until I read the first book of Genesis, chapter 2. This book of the Bible is like the Koran sura (chapter). At the end of Genesis chapter 2, I was so curious that I wanted to read it to you right now. "God created Adam and Eve, and they were created naked and had no shame."

Jim's comment came swiftly: "So what?" Hocine continued on. In Genesis 3, this perfectly shameless couple ate from the forbidden tree, sinned against Allah, and brought shame to themselves and to Allah. What did Allah do? He talked to Adam and Eve, now amazingly, in their shame and dishonor and tragic defilement.

Allah asked, "Where are you, Adam?" "Adam, who told you that you had nakedness?" Allah even told Adam and Eve, as they were expelled from the beautiful garden, that they would crush the tail of the serpent/jinn and that Allah would break into pieces the head of the same serpent of curses and Satan. Allah said, "Eve, you will bear children in pain, and Adam will have to plow the land, full of weeds until you sweat with fatigue." Allah, as He gave consequences for the sin, gave the promise, a spoken promise, of crushing the head of the darkness of Satan. That's partnership, and that's Allah speaking to Adam and Eve in a state of defilement and darkness. Jim, Allah wants to speak to you even now.

My thoughts, recounted Jim, was that I wanted to kill Pastor Hocine, to shut him up forever. But this was not my mission. Effectively, Hocine invited me to tear up the Holy Koran and read the Holy Bible, with Allah speaking. My head was going through a psychosis as I was losing contact with reality as I knew it. I had aberrant mental experiences through almost the whole complex and catatonic expressions of impaired insight and borderline paranoia. My mental state was riven with conflicting thoughts that made me want flight, to fight, and I fell into a deep sleep on Hocine's couch, utterly unable to cope. I slept for five hours, waking to a full spread of lamb on the dining table. I was very thirsty and seemed to stare into the emptiness of life. I might have well been drugged. How can I write all this to Cig? How do I get back on my feet? In every way! I'm lost, I'm captive, I'm torn up, and Hocine did me no harm.

Dear Cig,

I had my Chaoui visit with Pastor Hocine. He is a man of power and kindness, and rather in opposition to the Holy Koran, like all followers of Isa. I do not recommend any further visits to Hocine. His thinking is beyond anything we've seen up to this point. I'm afraid of this man, but I'm not sure why. He left a deposit on my soul

70

that has to be examined. My recommendation is that we do not send a report to headquarters on Hocine. They may ask for more details. I'm swamped with so many conflicts right now that I could never answer a full summation of my visit. Like the Vandals and Roman invaders were held in abeyance by the Chaouis and their mountainous region, so too do these people have some power to keep us at arm's length. Destroy any communication on this issue before it reaches headquarters in Somalia.

Chapter 12

The Problem Throughout Has Never Been God's Problem

We do personal evangelism because it is the highly contextualized strategy that was developed to plant the gospel into individualized cultures. Since Western nations are individualized, North Americans and Europeans have primarily been reached through personal evangelism. Since it worked in our lives, we assume it will work with everyone else. But what if their culture is not individualistic?

Luke reveals that Lydia "and the members of her household were baptized" (Acts 16:15). In response to the jailor's question, "Sirs, what must I do to be saved?" He was told, "Believe in the Lord Jesus, and you will be saved—you and your household." Then they spoke the word of the Lord to him and to all the others in his house…then immediately he and all his family were baptized…he was filled with joy because he had come to believe in God—he and his whole family" (Acts 16:31-34).

We have found when believers go to the least-reached people groups in cross-cultural ministry, there are often tragic results. The family turns against this new believer and throws them out of the household for being deceived by this foreign ideology. They hate Christians for "brainwashing" their son or daughter. They refuse to hear the gospel because it has brought them such excruciating pain. And then some believers quote passages that make it sound like God takes great pleasure in setting children against their parents.

Rest assured, the gospel entails challenges to any culture. It presents obstacles to human religions. But that is not what has just happened. A strategy was employed that withheld the gospel from the rest of the family. A divide-and-conquer strategy was used. (It is not that in a highly individualized culture, but it is in the rest of the world.) As a side note, the best time for a church to plant a new church is when it is new. Older churches want buildings, etc. (Acts 19:26).

I have found that when a Person of Peace is discipled through a process of facilitating their family's discovery of God, they are learning to share the gospel as quickly as they hear it. By discipling an insider who is already trusted by the family/affinity group, we find many insiders realize they, too are able to spread the good news. At every gathering, they are asked who they know who needs to hear that day's text. When they finally come back asking if they can bring their brother, cousin, or friend, they are coached in starting a new group that discovers the Lord. The process intentionally raises up disciple-makers, not just learners.

A tough but true word is as follows: Western culture has the content of the Biblical message but rarely has the context. Examples: the demonic man with chains; a man lowered down from a roof; a Samaritan woman who found "the Christ" and shared her Savior with her entire village.

73

Jesus' ministry rarely took place in the Synagogue.

Djamila was the worship leader in our church in Paris. She lived in Oran, Algeria. She took a bus to Oran only to find a Christian sitting opposite her who gave her some gospel literature. She thought very little of it. Then came a teenage youth gathering in the forest. She heard a speaker in the forest and then took a long walk in the forest. She gave her life to Christ in a wonderful way. Her mother heard about it and took her to the police. There the police walked them home, mother, daughter, and the policeman. He warned her never to tell another person about this and change her life to being a follower of Jesus. When Djamila got home, all hell broke loose. Her father rejected her and would not let her eat at the table, but he rejected her fully. (Was this the case of a whole family needing to become followers of Christ first of all?) A friend of Djamila knocked on the door to meet with her friend Djamila. No, her mother said, Djamila died. But Djamila was upstairs, reading her Bible. She heard all the lies of her mother. Her reading was "for me to live is Christ, to die is gain." This made her heart swell with joy unspeakable. She now felt she was loved eternally as she accepted the rejection as part of the package. Six years later, her father finally accepted and yearned for his dear daughter and then came to Christ, along with the mother as well. It was a long six years, but worth the wait. Jesus brought Djamila into His precious family and the family into His precious arms.

You can't make persecution fair. Satan will not allow it. Crucify your arrogance and learn humility as we sit at the feet of persecuted Christians. Please try to find persecuted or formerly persecuted Christians, even if you have to travel abroad to meet them on your vacation, and ask them questions about their survival and way of victory in Jesus. They have true Bible knowledge. (Acts 2, 3) shows the events of Pentecost, where 5,000 were saved and baptized, after which a great persecution arose. They fled Jerusalem and found even more persecution. I, Don, was fired and expelled from two missionary agencies. It hurt, but it was God's will for me to see if I would be crushed or if I would follow after Jesus stronger than ever. I did the latter. Where is the pressure on us coming from to remain silent? It is a form of persecution by closing off people from coming to Jesus.

"You can't seriously let lost people lead Bible studies!" is one response we hear. "There aren't lost people who are willing to lead a Bible study" is another assumption. Both reflect a failure to understand what a Person of Peace is. The lost who facilitates a Bible study is always a Person of Peace.

A Person of Peace is someone God prepares to serve as a bridge builder to their household or ethnic group and followers of Jesus. This person is already looked to as a leader, so we are not putting a lost person into a leadership position. We do equip this person to facilitate a Discovery Bible study. The coaching is done through a relationship that has begun around the spiritual

75

openness of this person. We have met this person by being "overtly spiritual without being obnoxiously religious." We openly point to God and what we are learning about Him and His expectations for our lives as we interact with people. Our purpose for these comments is to identify and connect with Persons of Peace. After we find them (or they find us), then a relationship is built that leads to the point of willingness to lead their circle of influence in a discovery process.

Another part of our Western culture that shaped our evangelistic strategies is our assumption that everyone here knows God and just needs to know Jesus. How people view God directly shapes how they hear the phrase "Son of God." When we fail to help them discover God's character as the Creator who calls men into a relationship and establishes a sacrificial system, then many of the descriptions of Jesus have no context to be deeply meaningful. We are obligated to include the story of Creation. Then our discipleship will be sure to help these new believers to be grounded in God's self-revelation so they can know how to disciple "disciple-makers."

Stop spending your time frustrating people who do not want to hear the gospel (yet), and start using your time looking for the lost people God is preparing. Share only where Jesus has prepared someone's heart to hear. Start with a Person of Peace (Luke 10: 6).

Some Persons of Peace are open to spiritual things because of things God has been doing in their lives for a long time. Note that Cornelius's prayers and helping the poor had caught Gods attention (Acts 10:4). Lydia was gathered with a group of women for prayer along the river (Acts 16:13). By contrast, though, God used remarkable circumstances to open the heart of the Philippian jailer (Acts 16:22-34). Paul's authentic spiritual conversions resulted in these two later encounters. But, sometimes, like with Cornelius, the Person of Peace finds us! It is an incredible joy to be God's speaker to a prepared heart.

If you are called to reach a city, it will require you to focus on a few to reach the many. Duplicate this several times and equip them to duplicate it, too, and you have the means to reach the town or city. There is still another element that should not be overlooked. The people you disciple should be seen by the target audience as insiders. Indigenous family heads are the best means to reach people groups who still have family-based systems.

In (Acts 10), Cornelius is an excellent example of a Person of Peace. He spends the three days between when he sends for Peter and his arrival gathering the people he influences and has them ready to listen to anything God tells them to do. God's spirit still prepares people like this in our world. God wants the nations to come to know Himself. His Son modeled for us a strategy of going slow in order to go fast. Discipling disciplers needs to become our strategy.

Chapter 13

Crossing Cultures Need Specialized Tools In God's Tool Kit

Did you ever wonder why the New Testament has four gospels? Please say, Yes. Each is an accurate presentation of the good news of Jesus for four different cultural groups. So much for "our one size fits all" idea. With drastically different worldviews, Matthew presents Jesus to the Jewish background believers. Mark presents Jesus to the Roman worldview. Luke presents Jesus for the Gentile background believers (and unbelievers). John presents Jesus for Eastern worldview peoples who were conducting their trading excursions into the province of Asia. Note where the kingdom of heaven and where the kingdom of God is used. Why is this the case?

The Jesus film has met with more success in Muslim African regions than in most of Asia. A young Cambodian church planter told a friend he knew why. "The Jesus Film uses the wrong gospel. If it used John's gospel instead of Luke's, it would be more fruitful here," he suggested. Of course, Jesus lived and discipled in a far different culture than our Western world. His life was lived with people with worldviews much more like those of sub-Saharan Africa and rural China than ours.

Now we have The Chosen, which acts out in a visual and almost oral method that touches hearts and minds of many cultures. There are some negative points that must be stated. Simply put, the more "churched" people are, the more likely they are resistant to reaching out cross-culturally. They already have their own cultural and religious way of doing things in an inviolable manner. I was broadly chastised by a woman in France who was part of our first French church and one of the top French prayer leaders. I asked a guitarist from Bulgaria, Michael, whom I met after my wallet was stolen. He called me to say he found my driver's license and credit cards in the trash bin as he was scavenging for food. I invited him to our church and, knowing he was an excellent guitarist, put him on the stage with the other worship leaders. The French prayer leader was horrified because she thought he, being an unbeliever, could bring demons into our church through his guitar playing. Sadly, at the time, I knew nothing about frontline acceptance and opening people to our church by loving acceptance. He got to the US eventually and said he was doing well and driving a taxi in Las Vegas.

In our reaching out in an intercultural fashion, we can fall into culture shock, which is the disorientation we experience when all the cultural maps and religious guidelines we learned as children no longer work. Reaching into a new culture, much of our old knowledge is useless, if not misleading. We can become overwhelmed by constantly having to face confusing situations and the strain of learning a new way of life that relates to other-cultural people.

My son lived in Mauritania for a year and ate so little and drank "coffee" made with burned tree roots and served as a sort of coffee. When he came down to Senegal for a conference, he couldn't feel comfortable with the huge amount of food available everywhere. He had a personal crisis and couldn't face real coffee and an "embarrassing" amount of food on each plate. He had to re-adjust from a minimalist and poor culture to more than "plenty enough." His appearance was so drawn and slimmed down that his smile was just a lot of teeth, with minor facial muscles. I could not take his picture to send to my wife.

We will have to re-establish ourselves in our home culture until we learn truly become bi-cultural, which is good, even ideal, as long as we are not retreating to our safe zone to avoid the strains of cross-cultural ministry. People know if you are a temporary cross-cultural worker and denying interculturalism, where you find your peace wherever the Lord leads you into another culture. In France, our most shocking words from visiting Americans is, "Isn't that quaint?"

Heartbreak sets in when we share our stories with people of our home culture, things that seemed so extravagant and unique in a world of need. People at home may soon lose interest in our stories and turn to more important topics of conversation—changes in the latest models of cars, politically motivated school board decisions, sports, or even inflation news.

We even find it hard to relate to our friends and relatives at home because they will not listen, or they will listen politely but do not seem to understand what we are trying to say. Our frustration is intensified by the fact that all this is so unexpected. We are out of step with the lifestyles that once seemed so important but now seem so self-centered. May I note the obvious? Cross-cultural ministry is costly, necessary, and can be a source of wounding. There is risk involved unless the people you report back to are your sending team, prayer team, or heart-to-heart support people.

Ephesians 3: 31-32 can be taken apart to refine our character so that we can be equipped to be cross-cultural capable:

1. I will live up to my calling to a righteous life.

2. In humility, I will put up with a lot from the people I love in God's family.

3. I will work hard to hold on to the peace God's underlying Spirit creates.

4. I will stay humble regarding the gifts of the Spirit given from Jesus.

5. I will recognize only Jesus earned the right to give the gifts of the Spirit.

6. I will follow His example of humbly leaving heaven to become a man.

7. I will recognize God exalted Him for His humility, as he will exalt you.

8. I will accept the fact that Jesus set the kingdom up according to His purpose.

9. I will build up the body by using my gifts in serving others.

10. I will work for God's goal of mature faith in Jesus.

11. I will measure up to the standard of Jesus.

12. I will seek maturity because it protects us from the damaging effects of false teachers.

13. I will lovingly speak the truth like Jesus so we grow to be more and more like our head.

14. I will remember it takes all of us working together under His guidance to be built up in love—each must do their part.

15. I will choose mature thinking, rather than thinking in the old futile ways.

16. I will keep my heart soft by doing whatever God calls me to do.

In the Scriptures, we find that God changes the people he calls by giving them a new identity, challenging them to live up to that sense of self-definition, and empowering their new walk. Because our relationship with Jesus makes us "holy," we are called to live holy lives. Here we see the connection between "indicatives" and "imperatives" in Paul's writings. In the first half of most of his letters, he discusses the identity of people "in Christ." The second half shows how that new identity in Christ changes the way we are to behave and determines to a great extent what we do.

Jesus wants all His disciples to recognize that following Him means we begin to search for the people God wants to be transformed, oriented toward Jesus, and eventually matured into new and welcoming church plants. Jesus said His disciples would be like their master. Are you like Him?

We in the Western world experience what some call SADD or "Spiritual Attention Deficit Disorder." Television is rapidly eroding our capacity to be attentive. We long for interruptions and will create them if necessary. Due to this condition, we are unable to meditate on the Word of God. We will pay men well to chew up the Word and spit it into our mouths, so we only have to swallow it. We become enraged by those who would dare to expect us to do our own reading, our own meditating, our own study, and our own cross-cultural ministry to other ethnic non-Christian peoples. Rather learn to revere the Lord, carefully obey His commandments, and meditate on His Word to avoid being "Sunday morning Christians."

While the same gospel is preached to Jewish and Gentile communities, cultural diversity existed, which did not conflict with the teaching about Jesus' death, burial, and resurrection. Remember, Paul rebuked Peter to his face for his failure to uphold this in Antioch. A close reading of Acts and Paul's letters reveals he was not into the franchise control business. Churches were established quickly, indigenous leaders were appointed, and Paul moved on to regions. Yes, he continued to mentor and teach these leaders, but Paul's methodology was not an edict but a calling for leaders to make the right choices based on what they knew of Jesus. Paul's own example and his reasoning with his leaders came from letters and messengers. Paul did not discuss "handing the church over to the locals" at some distant point when they were his clones. His practice acknowledged the continuing work of the Holy Spirit in the lives of these believers. He knew they would rapidly mature as they put into practice the things they already knew.

Dirty Cop Scrutiny In Your Tool Kit

A large number of action movies are thrillers because they feature the exposure of dirty cops who wear the badge but work for the mob or a criminal organization. What does this have to do with your tool kit in becoming a cross-cultural or intercultural ministering agent of Christ to ethnic peoples of this world? I tossed and turned last night. I could not sleep until I could write this as part of the critical tools to be effective in your life in the cross-cultural world.

Jesus said in (Matt 7:21-24) the following, "Not everyone who says to Me, 'Lord, Lord,' shall enter the kingdom of heaven, but he who does the will of My Father in heaven. Many will say to Me in that day, 'Lord, Lord, have we not prophesied in Your name, cast out demons in Your name, and done many wonders in Your name?' And then I will declare to them, 'I never knew you; depart from Me, you who practice lawlessness!' "Therefore whoever hears these sayings of Mine, and does them, I will liken him to a wise man who built his house on the rock."

The "dirty cop" term signifies having a Christian life and confession but a complex and evil heart which has very little to do with following Jesus completely and thoroughly. Another way of understanding this is that human beings can hold Christian commitment and non-Christian actions in their lives and in their minds at the same time. For this reason, I am not very confident with "confessional churches," which consider Christian commitment a simple result of a word of confession.

The workers in Matthew 7 were doing godly works, extraordinary miracles, and even prophecies without letting Christ know and thus have a relationship with Christ. Why does God allow huge churches to continue to grow under a pastoral leadership who has a private life of gross immorality? Why do some Christians who are not pastors continue to live immoral lives and yet present themselves as top-rated missionary leaders with great effectiveness? We call these Christians "divided heart Christians."

The reason God allows divided heart Christians to continue to be successful is for the sake of His word being sown and non-Christians being converted, and Christians strengthened in their faith. Jonah was against the gentile, pagan Ninevites, and self-absorbed—but God used him in a great way to preach to the people of wicked Nineveh. Balaam was an evil prophet, yet God spoke with him and showed himself to him. Solomon was the instrument to bring the Queen of Sheba to the Lord. She may have traveled from Yemen. Solomon became a great writer of books of the Bible but turned to demonic idols. These evil gestures and characters still had a walk with God because even a donkey can be used to speak the word of the Lord, as it did in the story of Balaam.

It is inconceivable for a person with a divided heart to be able to reach out in cross-cultural ministry. Eventually, sin will be exposed and judged now and into eternity. How can a person be set free from having a divided heart? According to Matthew 7, the answer is to not just know the Lord but to let the Lord know you. In (Psalms 19:7-11), "The law of the Lord is perfect, converting the soul: the testimony of the Lord is sure, making wise the simple." This requires not just Bible reading but an ongoing relationship with Christ with constant contact and obedience with Him to show you deliverance from debilitating and dark temptations.

David was most frustrated when he asked, "How can a young man keep his way pure? By keeping it according to Your word (Ps. 119:9). Paul battled with a pure heart in Romans 7, finding that he did wrong by the lure of the flesh and battled to be free. He found freedom in Romans 8, by the walk in the Spirit of God in Christ Jesus. Examine yourselves to see if you are in the faith constantly. "Examine yourselves to see whether you are in the faith; test yourselves. Do you not realize that Christ Jesus is in you—unless, of course, you fail the test? (2 Cor. 13:5). Ask the Lord morning, noon, and night for Jesus' life to become infused into your life. This alone is our life's sustenance. Our soulish desires need to be conquered and put to rest daily.

Chapter 14

Musa Shares How Cig and Jim Found How Jesus Cast Out Darkness Powerfully

Cig, I got an invitation from Samir, to eat with him and hear his story. It had to be at a restaurant since he didn't want his wife Asma to hear the story. This involves travel again. Tabelbala is a town and commune between Béchar and Tindouf in southwestern Algeria and is the capital, and only significant settlement, of the Daïra of the same name, encompassing most of the southwestern half of Béchar Province. That's where I'm heading, to Tabelbala, which is a unique oasis area where the water level is high enough for agriculture. These are Korandje-speaking people who are close to Morocco and to Tindouf. It is the only town in Algerian where the total population of 3,000 speak neither Arabic nor Berber languages, but rather Korandje. I have to fly into Tindouf and drive 70 km up north to Tabelbala. Samir, a Jesus follower, heard of us and wanted a meeting, which I could not deny. They have four mosques in town, with two more being built.

Samir, a goat rancher, who has a large portion of the 9,949 goats in town, welcomed me warmly. Warmly is the key word since it is so hot there that 46 degrees is typical for July. I was greeted with dates, and later fed with goat meat and grains from the agricultural work. We had couscous and goat milk, and goat cheese.

Jim asked Samir why we had to meet in a restaurant and not in his house, though he was a follower of Isa

(Jesus). How did you become a follower of Isa (Jesus) in this remarkable oasis anyway? Samir replied, "I'm not the pastor of the church here, which is very small and secretive. But the church was planted by a non-Algerian, someone from another country, from Germany, I think. He came here and told people he was a Hanifi Christian. We know from the Koran that a hanif or hanifi is a person with their faith based on the faith of Abraham. So we invited him into our homes. He was very skilled and kind.

"He brought us a hospitality gift and then announced being a hanifi Christian. We were stunned since none of us could say that we had attained the faith of Abraham to become a Hanifi. So we had to listen to him. He could speak French, so we found a translator for him, someone who could translate his words into Korandje. He listened to us before he spoke. We had so many questions about him and then began to trust him. "It wasn't my house, but I heard everything since people are oral here and memorize every word that this German spoke. So I heard of the meeting of the first-ever Hanifi Christian."

Jim asked, "What did he say next?"

Samir continued, "He told the story of Jesus healing the blind man. We know of no healing by the prophet Mohammed. So we memorized the story of the healing and recited it to everyone we met. Then he asked what the story says about Jesus. Everyone said that if we call to Jesus, he will heal us too. But he went on to ask the strangest question we had ever heard.

Jim, "What was that question?"

Samir, "He asked if he could clean the house. Was this a joke? The house, full of people, asked what he meant. He said that Tabelbala was known as a town of monuments and Islamic saints, some buried, some as statues that people touch for Baraka power. He said that if there were curses or spirits of the jinn in any part of the house where the people met, he would clean them out in the name of Jesus, the Isa that we spoke of. And he did it. Every room, the bathroom, the closets, the kitchen, the sitting room, even to the point of walking around the house and proclaiming the name of Jesus. We knew this was a new source of power with more strength than our Marabout, who just added more curses to us. The whole house, full of people, erupted in jubilation and shouts of Isa, Isa, Isa. They all committed themselves to Isa, Lord of life."

Jim, "Why are we then meeting with dates and goat milk in this restaurant?"

Jim, Samir noted this happened eight years ago. We now have fruitful agriculture, very reproductive goats, and larger dates as well. But I can't tell my wife. If she finds out, she will gossip among the women to the point of the militant Muslims coming out to my home to arrest me. Actually, many, many men are followers of Jesus but won't tell their wives since they gossip. My wife Maria knows that I don't beat her anymore. I'm a totally loving and transformed person, but I dare not confide in her. The secret is that we have no curses on our home any longer, and I'm the hidden follower of Isa.

Jim became agitated. Ok, it's true that Mohammed never healed anyone. But he is the last prophet, so you need to get rid of this Isa crap and come back to the final prophet, the Kalimet of Allah, Mohammed. He is the prophet of God, have you forgotten that he was the last prophet? Samir's answer came straight forward and with blazing boldness. Jim, I was transformed by Isa, curses were broken by him, he was the healer, and now my life with Maria is fully a miracle wonder. If I was lost and perishing, then saved by this prophet Isa, why do I need a "last prophet" that you say won't heal or even speak? I don't need a late arrival to the party to tell me to beat my wife again. This is not your Algeria, Jim.

Cig,

Samir came right out with it all and took me to a restaurant where he had so much to share that I came away feeling like we all got too much sun in this god-forsaken place called Thabelbala. Samir would disagree with the place being called god-forsaken since this follower of Isa (Jesus) has secrets that may go with him to the grave. His wife doesn't know he is a follower of Isa, and much of the town has places to meet that do not draw attention to their meeting. I had to go to the mosque on Friday to face the demons on my right and left shoulders, knowing that they will keep coming back with fire from hell the jinn sent by Allah to keep us in discipline. Then along comes this German teacher who permanently expels all curses and jinn/demonic darkness on every corner of the house where he taught. My mosque's Salat prayers seem to be again and again the same thing. The teacher cleaned every spirit in the name of Isa. This may be a fake way of blinding people who die in hell seven times hotter. The trickery goes on and on, and people are flocking to this new type of Marabout follower of Isa. It may end with upheaval on the streets when people find out that the Religion is the only way to satisfy Allah, who of course, sends the jinn/demons to attack us and prove us to be worthy of paradise. Tabelbala remains so remote that getting there takes a day. Food is abundant in this oasis, not far from Tinndouf.

Chapter 15

Is The Bible Above Culture?

Many people believe that the Bible is so unique and universal in its truths that it is above culture. My reply is that only a mono-cultural person could make this statement,

Many cultures, rather, have bridges to Christ from similar beliefs to Biblical beliefs. For example, God reveals much about Himself, such as His "eternal power and divine nature" (Rom. 1:20), but even this is "suppressed" or consciously denied by godless people (Rom. 1:18 NIV). A culture may reflect God's principles of hospitality to strangers (Ex. 22:21; Lev. 19:10; Heb. 13:2), for instance. It may have strong taboos against embarrassing anyone ("face" saving, (1 Cor. 13:4).

We can even use non-Christian beliefs. The Greek poet Aratus wrote accurately, "We are his God's offspring." (Acts 17:28). Paul referred to Zeus. Jesus declared that the cultural assertions of Samaritans regarding the place to worship were absolutely wrong (John 4:19-22).

Puzzling Scriptures may reflect culturally specific issues which were more relevant to a particular time and place. Not a few, for example, believe that a woman should teach men in the church today, despite 1 Tim. 2:12, since, we are told, women were domineering a local church, and it was simply a local problem, confined to one time and culture. However, Paul's reasoning in his prohibition goes all the way back to Adam and Eve, to the origin of gender relationships, which suggests a larger application of his words (1 Tim. 2:13-14). The issue of polygamy is similar. Those opposing it go to Gen. 2:24, where one man and one woman become "one flesh" (cf. Matt. 19:5), which is the clearest and most authoritative teaching of women. In thousands of ways, Christians have been salt and light in culture, exposing darkness and preserving the good.

God is both able and willing to reveal errors in our understanding (Phi. 3:15). The Word of God "is living and active, sharper than any double-edged sword, it penetrates even to dividing soul and spirit, joints and marrow; it judges the thoughts and attitudes of the heart." (Heb. 4:12). However, understanding God's mind involves nonconformity to the prevailing unchristian worldview (Rom. 12:2). A culture will be as Christian as its people have been permeated with biblical truth.

Women should have long hair (I Cor. 11) to be considered godly. We see this as culturally specific, where immoral women cut their hair short. Our summary here is that there are culturally specific issues in the Bible that do not discount the infallibility of the Word. It does show that the Bible is not above culture but able to interweave itself into the prevailing culture and disclose God's relationship with His offspring and Salvation in His Son.

Though The Bible Is Not Above All Culture, God Loves All Peoples

God is intentionally involved in cross-cultural ministry. Because Christians are to go to every ethnic group, this implies not only the mandate but its feasibility. In fact, Christ Himself accompanies us (Matt. 28:19-20, cf. Heb. 13:5-6). In the Old Testament, Christ was to be a "light for the Gentiles" (Is. 42:6-7). "It is too small a thing for you to be my servant to restore the tribes of Jacob and bring back those of Israel I have kept. I will also make you a light for the Gentiles, that you may bring my salvation to the ends of the earth." (Is.49:6, NIV). At Pentecost, the divisive effects of the dispersion through language confusion (linguistic separation due to the sin of pride) at Babel (Gen. 11:4-9) was momentarily overcome. "Jews from every nation under heaven . . . heard them speaking in his own language." (Acts 2:5-6).

This underscores the decisive barrier that language is to cross-cultural ministry. We need to be able to communicate in the "heart" language of the people to be best understood. Even a riot was calmed when Jews heard Paul speak in their own tongue (Acts 22;2). The salvation of 3,000 at Pentecost included the same cosmopolitan gathering (Acts 2:41). The church, from its inception, has been multicultural and transcultural. The church in its final form will include those purchased by Christ's blood "from every tribe and language and people and nation." (Rev. 5:9). The barrier to sharing the Gospel with non-Jews took extraordinary measures to overcome, including angelic visitation, visions, and providential timing (Acts 10:3, 11, 19-20).

Most cultures tend toward ethnocentrism, toward a prejudicial preference of their own culture over all others.

Ethnocentrism is prejudicial because the strengths of other cultures are often not appreciated. The attitude that "we are the people" prevails. This pride is perhaps the most tremendous among those with the least experience with other cultures.

Culture may be defined as the particular solutions to the needs of life adopted by a group of people. It rests upon beliefs. The deepest beliefs and assumptions about the world, including values, perspectives, taboos, and behaviors, constitute one's worldview. A worldview constitutes a cognitive grid through which perceptions are interpreted. Typically this worldview cannot be articulated by the holder since it is taken for granted and is so deeply ingrained from birth. A person wearing glasses, for instance, doesn't notice the lenses, yet they are unique to the needs of the wearer and would not help most others to see properly. One's worldview can be illuminated through contact with contrasting cultures. It can be judged as "right" or "wrong" by the absolute standard of the Bible. Otherwise, a culture can be judged to be relatively more or less efficient in dealing with its unique environment. Worldview can also be illuminated by the "deep structures" inherent in language. It is common wisdom that to understand a people, their language needs to be comprehended in trying to discover the worldview of an ethnic group.

Possible explanations for a specific behavior, such as spending great sums for a wedding, are considered. As other "unusual" behaviors are observed, perhaps throwing an expensive party when someone prospers financially, explanations are sought which explain as many of the "unusual" behaviors as possible. That explanation, the intersection of the largest number of adequate answers to behavior, would be a key to the worldview.

India has an extraordinary death rate among newly born baby girls. The proverb they use is that "you can't take the fruit off the tree, but you can take it when it falls to the ground." In other words, they are against abortion, but once the baby girl is born, you can end her life without hindrance or conscience. The reason for destroying baby girls is that when they grow up and seek marriage, the needed dowry is so huge that the father and mother are driven into grinding poverty, from which they can never recover. The simple answer is to lower the size of the dowry to a minimal amount of money.

But this is not according to the Indian culture or worldview.

THE BIBLE IS MULTI-CULTURAL

The Bible is a cross-cultural training document. It has the only absolutes that we possess. A member of any culture can use it safely to relate both to God and to fellow humans. Commonalities outweigh differences among people. We are more alike than dissimilar. The image of God rests on all people

96

(Gen. 1:27). All people have a longing for eternity in some form, for instance (Eccles. 3:11). God has given people consciences, which reflect another attribute shared with God, morality (Rom. 2:14-15). Humans also love, which reflects God (1 John 4:8). People also have an aesthetic sense--we appreciate sunsets and art. We enjoy beauty because God made that beauty. He himself is beautiful (Ps. 27:4). He is extravagant with that beauty, creating flowers that none will ever see but Himself. We have highly developed symbolic language. The principles of Scripture are intended by God to be used by persons of any culture in relation to other persons of any other culture or subculture. Otherwise, it would be suitable for only Near Eastern and Greco-Roman cultures.

The Gospel can bridge each cultural separation. However, the existence of these divisions creates challenges both within and among cultures. Typical differences are magnified by sin and exploited by Satan. This is so among Christians, as well as non-Christians. Fallen people join fallen societies. It is possible for certain sins to dominate a city, as sexual perversion dominated Sodom and Gomorrah (Jude 1:7). Intellectual pride seems to have overtaken Athens in the first century A.D. (Acts 17:18). The Assyrians were known for their cruelty (Nahum 3:19). Such strongholds of sin require divinely powerful weapons to destroy them. Among such weapons is prayer (2 Cor. 10:4-5). Conversion of individuals will result in the change of societies composed of individuals. A Christian is a "new creation" following a new master, with new goals and values (2 Cor. 5:17; Col. 1:13). But even Christian churches can have strongholds of sin, as the letters to five of the seven churches in Revelation reveal (Rev. 2-3). Ephesus lacked love for God (Rev. 2:4); Thyatira apparently tolerated sexual immorality (Rev. 2:20); Sardis was complacent; (Rev. 2:2-3); Laodicea was proud (Rev. 3:17).

Not only are individuals fallen historically through Adam (Rom. 5:12), but they are actively dominated by a wicked ruler, Satan. "The whole world is under the control of the evil one." (1 John 5:19). God's superior power is evident, however. Jesus keeps God's people safe (1 John 5:18). Satan's defeat is decreed (Rev. 20:10). Conversion robs Satan of a subject, so evangelism is spiritual warfare. Considering the enemy, we can do nothing apart from Christ (John 15:5). Satan has his subjects in supernatural blindness (2 Cor. 4:4). Christians are advised to wear the full armor of God (Eph. 6:10-18) so that they can "be strong in the Lord and in his mighty power." (Eph. 6:10). Cross-cultural ministry compounds the normal problems of evangelism, increasing possible misunderstanding. Because of the supernatural nature of resistance to the Gospel, the Holy Spirit must come in convicting power upon the unsaved (John 16:8). This is technically an awakening, in contrast to a revival.

One hundred years have elapsed since the last worldwide revival. The most prudent mission strategy is prayer for the Holy Spirit to come upon both the Church and the lost in great power. Generally, a revival results in zealous new missionaries, as with the East Africa Revival, begun in 1930.

DEGREES IN CROSS-CULTURAL MINISTRY

Acts 1:8 is suggestive of degrees in cross-cultural ministry. For a Jew, Jerusalem represents mono-cultural ministry or ministry to one's own culture. Judea represents one's own culture in another locale. However, even within one's culture are pockets of those with a different subculture. In America, ministry to "hyphenated-Americans" is cross-cultural in nature. Ministry in Samaria is analogous to such a cross-cultural ministry. Samaritans were intermingled Jewish/Canaanite stock and had a paganized Judaism (2 Kings 17:26-34). "Even while these people were worshipping the Lord, they were serving their idols." (2 Kings 17:41). This is equivalent to Christo-paganism, on the order of "Mariolatry" in Roman Catholicism. Usually, the basic language is the same, although of a different dialect (such as Black English is to English.") The extent of Christ's call is to the end of the earth" (Acts 1:8). Language and culture are entirely different from those of the missionary. A South American missionary who goes to India is an example. Linguistic gifts are needed for ministry. Historic hostilities can increase the distance between the missionary culture and the target culture, as the Jewish/Samaritan situation, and as Whites ministering to African Americans illustrate.

INCARNATION
The most significant "cultural" gap ever bridged was when the eternal Logos (John 1:1) became the infant Jesus. He emptied Himself, voluntarily limiting the exercise of aspects of His divine glory (Phil. 2:6-8). Jesus, "Who being in very nature God, did not

consider equality with God something to be grasped, but made himself nothing, taking the very nature of a servant, being made in human likeness." (Phil. 2:6-7). This incarnational principle of cross-cultural ministry is probably the dominant model today in evangelical missions. Jesus "did not come to be served, but to serve, and to give his life as a ransom for many." (Mark 10:45). Jesus, who as God was the agent of creation, became a humble member of humanity He made (Col. 1:16). Paul wrote of such sacrifice: "Your attitude should be the same as that of Christ Jesus." (Phil. 2:5). So service is a cross-cultural way of life. Service bonds us to the recipient (2 Cor. 9:14).

It creates bridges, as did the flesh of the God-man. This identification with the "target" people was illustrated by Paul. "I have become all things to all men so that by all possible means I might save some." (1 Cor. 9:22b). "Though I am free and belong to no man, I make myself a slave to everyone, to win as many as possible." (1 Cor. 9:19). Circumcision illustrates this principle. Paul had Timothy, who had a Jewish mother, circumcised, in order to be found acceptable to the Jews (Acts 16:3). The principle of "contextualization," or the principle of making the Gospel as relevant to a given ethnic people as possible, without compromising the biblical truth, is illustrated by this circumcision. However, accommodation to a people halts if it is in conflict with Scripture. Paul refused to circumcise Titus so that it would not give the message that a Christian had to first observe the Law (Gal. 2:2-5). Normally circumcision is not an issue (1 Cor. 7:18-19). Incarnational ministry is flexible, without compromise. What exactly "compromise" is has been problematic. What is the line between honoring a worshipping ancestor?

HOW FAR CAN WE COMPROMISE WITH PEOPLE OF OTHER CULTURES?

A missionary probably cannot completely identify with those served. This is due to differences in the mother tongue, worldview, education, and often economic level, having access to education and other North American resources. Ministries to the poor live in the slums of Manila to incarnate the Gospel to the poor. However, maintaining that complete cultural identification is not possible. For example, one may decide to keep one's engineering credentials current for use when needed. Once a week, one missionary was able to leave to gain perspective, strength, and Christian fellowship. This is not a criticism but illustrates that complete identification is probably not possible. One can make a strong case for the estrangement of missionary and host cultures because of economic distance. I advise identification economically with the host culture. However, if a missionary is on par with the people, he cannot minister because ministry costs money, unlike business, which also gains money from serving people. A worker will also have the power of personal networks. It is hard to deny, in any case, that a "compound" mentality puts distance between missionary and national. One resolution is to live at the level of those to whom we minister primarily. While God is interested in the Gospel for the poor (Luke 4:18), He desires missionaries to all the world, including the middle and upper classes, something extremely difficult for a missionary who identifies with the poor. God has

His people at all levels of society (whether official missionaries or not).

Chapter 16

Musa Relates The Story of Jim Spying To Analyze Muslim Conversion

Brahim is a hell brand, ripe for floods of darkness. I, Musa, told the story to Cig. He encouraged me to travel to Oran again, where some trouble was brewing. Going west, I arrived in Oran, the second city in Algeria, in population and even some tourism. It was a 30-minute flight to get there from Algiers.

A particularly dark cloud descended upon Oran just before I arrived, with a manhunt for Isa/Jesus followers who were incarcerated, some killed, and others tortured. Even badly injured, mostly Kabyle Berbers were denied medical help, and many just disappeared. I thought of this as a victory for the purging of Christians from our Islamic homeland in Oran. Until I met Nabil, that is a fervent Isa follower who was now wavering in his commitment to Christ.

Perfect, I thought. I will get two bangs for my buck. I'll get him back into Islam and, at the same time, find what causes Isa's followers to hesitate their leaving the Religion, Islam. Nabil is back in the Mosque again, doing his Salat Islamic prayers, though reading his Bible at home. I gained his confidence as a so-called neutral and pro-Isa follower, which was a lie. Nabil realized that if he continued meeting with other Isa (Jesus) brothers that he would be found out and, at the very minimum, denied a job, causing his family to starve. So he donned his hijab and made his commitment to Islam very apparent by only associating with Muslims and the local Imam. So I questioned him, both out of curiosity and to poison his waning commitment to Isa (Jesus). Nabil, "Why do Isa followers say they only serve one God, but in reality, they have this trinity of the Father, the Son, and the Mother?" Nabil called me an imbecile since the trinity has nothing to do with the Mother, but is a false Koranic teaching that no Isa follower believes. He weakened and said that to be honest, Christians have the one God almost separated into three parts because they don't know if they should pray to the Father, to the Son, or to the Holy Spirit. Nabil insisted on calling followers of Isa Christians since he is Kabyle. Kabyles like Western forms and names like the word "Christian." He said most Christians are mixed up and show it by saying, "Jesus told me..." or, "I have the power of the Holy Spirit," or "We are children of the Father." Jim, Christians are a mixed-up bunch with this one-God Trinity. Even Islam is more precise on only one God plus prophets like Moses and Jesus. I was watching a follower of Isa start to crack apart.

Nabil, "When you pray the Salat Islamic prayers, looking at your right and left shoulders, you are telling the jinn, demons, to leave you or to curse you forever. What do your Isa brothers tell you about ridding yourself of darkness?" Christian brothers usually say that Jesus took care to defeat the devil. But the curses are rarely addressed. We all carry a talisman, items of power, and things to ward off curses in our pockets as Christians.

I even went to a teaching conference in Tizzi. The master teacher was an American, myself. I stopped teaching and asked all 200 pastors present to put their power objects on his Holy Bible. (This was mentioned in detail above.) Nobody hesitated since this one teacher knew he could break all the curses in the name of Jesus. All 200 went forward and covered the Bible with shells and gri-gri Koranic verses of protection, as fully described above. Nobody teaches us to be aware of curses but to ignore them as forever gone. This shakes me as a Christian. Some Western missionaries came here saying that Christians could never have a devil/jinn curse. I'm hanging on by a thread, Jim. They don't know the power of rivers, rocks, Marabouts, shells, and Koranic verses tied around the neck. We have visions and dreams. Christians don't ask us about our visions. I feel so cut off. I saw the fools of Isa without the wisdom of Islam.

Nabil, "Why do you call Jesus the Son of God and make Allah into a sexual pervert with the Virgin Mary?" Jim, you may have lost your mind. You sound like a jackass that has been forced into carrying a burden that isn't yours to carry. You sound crazy. All Muslims call a whorish prostitute a son of haram or son of evil. You call fishermen sons of the sea. You call professional people as sons of their profession or trade. Jesus was called the Son of God before He was born as a baby from the Virgin Mary. I can show you from the Zabur, the Psalms, chapter 2, that God called Jesus His Son. Jim, if a prostitute is the son of haram, what does son mean? It means that she and the evil haram are identical. Jesus, as "Son of God" was the very identical person to Allah, God. Jim, stop repeating such silly teachings. You yourself use "son of" probably a dozen times a day to describe a person. My heart weakened when I found out that some Christians believe that Son of God means he was born a baby in Bethlehem. But they, too, are crass untrained, and untaught. But it further weakens my Christian faith. Nabil, "Will you come back to the Religion and stop all this questionable Isa confusion? The Brothers of Islam want you to follow the straightway of the Koran."

Jim, I'm in the mosque now to feed my family. The Muslims you want me to rejoin will kill me if I reveal I'm a Christian. Christians would never kill Muslims unless they converted to Jesus. I'm so tired of the sword, the vengeance, the cleansing of fornication by taking a bath. My Jesus is still my Savior in all my fear and confusion. I would die for Him, not for Islam. Good-bye Jim. This is not your Algeria.

Cig, write the above down. We're getting close to stopping the impure infidels from dishonoring and shaming Allah. Nabil seems locked up in the Mosque but won't deny his defiled ways of polluting himself and bringing curses on others by his hate-filled heart toward Allah. There is no mercy for him. Curses will befall him soon.

Highly organized, 17,000 Europeans and other foreigners have flown to Turkey as the latest additions, and we will soon decide which unit within al-Shabab for them to join.

Some show off their gymnastic skills to impress Sheik Ali Dhere. The recruits might remain regular fighters, become bomb-makers or work for the Amniyat, al-Shabab's elite intelligence network. But the most popular unit is the suicide brigade, and, believe it or not, there is a long waiting list. Only the best recruits will be accepted.

A secret that is mostly kept under wraps is that defections from al-Shabab are also rising. Though we conquered Ramadi because Allah sent a great sandstorm that allowed us to advance in the biting and blistering windy dust, the memory of Kenya has drawn down some of our forces.

More than 147 people have been killed in an attack on a college in eastern Kenya by the Somali-based Islamic extremists al-Shabaab, government officials have said. Scores were wounded in the April 2, 2015 attack, and four suspected attackers had been killed, Joseph Nkaissery, the interior minister, said. Five hundred students had been rescued, he said.

The minister ordered a dusk-to-dawn curfew in Garissa and in the nearby counties of Wajir, Tana River, and Mandera. Masked gunmen from al-Shabaab stormed into the university shortly after 5 am and then claimed to be holding an unknown number of Kenyan Christians hostage.

Cynically, Kenyan police offered a $220,000 bounty for Mohammed Mohamud, whom they believe, is the mastermind of the attack. We laugh at the millions we have in al-Shabab coffers. Toothpicks for a mastermind. Insulting. Most of the dead were Christians who pretended they were better than us. They have no beautiful women waiting for them in paradise. We are against modernization and education, and books—so the university was the perfect place to launch attacks against these Christians.

But the dilemma is that this butchery has caused a sort of reflux. Our recruits and even some hardened al-Shabab soldiers are defecting because they have a sort of soul that can't stand the wholesale blood-letting of 147 Christian students. This is why the Sha wanted Cig and me to find out why Jesus' followers were multiplying in Algeria. The dates are set for a full-scale march across Tunisia from Libya to degrade this Christian advance. Christians are Crusaders and marched upon us in 1095 at the urging of Pope Urban II. For 200 years, several hundred thousand Roman Catholic Crusaders marched against Islam with the reward of plenary indulgences from the Church. The Crusades, in turn, spawned medieval romance, philosophy, and literature. However, the crusades reinforced the connection between Western Christendom, feudalism, and militarism that ran counter to the "peace and truce of God" that Pope Urban had promoted.

We won't forgive them for this. Now is our al-Shabab answer, including an end to literature, books, and the arts. Death is our wish, not only to Christians but to non-practicing Muslims and, gloriously to us, to attain the caliphate and the reward of the jihad: beautiful women in paradise forever. The caliphate will welcome the return of the great Mahdi to judge non-Muslims, break all crosses, and kill all pigs. Strangely, many believe the great Mahdi is Jesus Christ, you know, the one proclaimed by the followers of Jesus we seek to undermine in Algeria. But defections are mounting apace of the Kenyan massacre among al-Shabab. Some of the al-Shabab jihadists still have a soul, you could say. The mystery remains as to why

Jesus followers in Algeria probably numbering 100,000, even though they say 50,000 to keep the authorities calm.

Cig and I are Algerian al-Shabab recruits, of course. It is driving me into a frenzy of mental torment at times, as I've said. Recruitment to al-Shabab, to get back to that, is similar to race-baiting in the USA. It's a clever evil to make people feel like victims, true or false, and that a sort of revenge has to rise up to avenge last week's or last century's wrongs. Then the race baiters run off with their intended prize, stardom, preeminence, sums of money, control of the government, and the weakening of society to the detriment of the mobs and thugs.

The similarity is too stunning for words. Here is a quote from an al-Shabab leader, "The Muslim people in Kenya should take up arms; Kenya should be attacked, its state should be destroyed. As is written in the Quran, when the disbelievers oppress by killing children and women... Allah has said if they punish you or hurt you, do to them like that which they did to you. By God's permission, we will fight Kenya, and we will concentrate our efforts in Kenya..."

Sheikh Fuad also tells us that most Al-Shabaab members operating within Kenya are of Kenyan origin and are victims of its government's policies towards Muslims. (Sound familiar?)

"We are training Muslim boys from Kenya who had been oppressed there, and we return them back there. The ones that we sent and killed your troops (in Mandera) are these; the ones we are going to send your way are much more than the ones we have already sent, by the permission of Allah…I end this by saying that we will move the war to Nairobi – and it is a promise we made to Allah"

Discrimination plays into the hands of Al-Shabaab, which uses stories of Muslim oppression in Kenya to recruit members and justify attacks in the country. Al-Shabaab's foreign operations arm is heavily populated by members of non-Somali ethnic backgrounds; this makes it operationally easier to insert these individuals into Al-Shabaab targets in neighboring countries.

Chapter 17

Your Culture and Other Religions Will Try to Influence You If You Don't Reach Out to Them Cross-Culturally

The above stories emphasize how other cultures will not remain silent but rather drill down to influence us if we are not proactive. Cross-cultural ministry is not only a nice side job but rather a lifeline to strengthen our own walk with God. Like muscle exercise, you use it or lose it, now in Christian lives.

A large group of cross-cultural workers was interviewed to determine the top five biggest and most vital steps to successful ministry. Here are the results:

1. The **importance of prayer was recognized as first place**. Paul's practice of praying for those he was discipling was clearly seen in the Ephesians texts. His conduct while in Ephesus and Miletus shows the importance of prayer in his church planting strategy.

2. **The role of obedience was mentioned as second**. This is especially evident in Paul's dialogue with the Ephesian elders in Acts 20, and it is also seen in the choice of Ephesian believers to destroy their magical stuff (Acts 19:18-19). We noted that Paul's desire that they know Jesus would have entailed behavior and not just head knowledge.

3. **The issue of spiritual warfare being part of church planting was noted as number 3**. The riot in Ephesus and Paul's words to the elders about them not seeing Him again were coupled with the "spiritual armor" text in Ephesians. There was the recognition that some would find the spread of the gospel has an adverse effect on their

income and would oppose the work. It was noted by some participants the importance of remembering that the war is not with "flesh and blood, but with principalities and powers" (Eph.6:12).

4. **The need to develop indigenous leaders was discussed as the fourth place of importance**. This insight was gained from Paul's dialogue with elders. It was also noted that Paul's conduct in Ephesus, during the time he taught the disciples in a rented school, showed the following. It shows him pouring himself into others. I also pointed out that Colossians and Philemon are additional letters Paul wrote to believers who lived in the province of Asia, and would be worthwhile for them to study in this context.

5. **The fundamental significance of having a servant's heart was examined last**. Paul's lifestyle was held up as an example for the elders to incorporate into their lives. His practice of tent-making was discussed as a way of looking at using a trade as a means of furthering the spread of the gospel. Some of the participants shared that there are times when such will be beneficial rather than a hindrance to their efforts to plant churches.

To continue your personal evaluation, consider these very small areas which really count before the Lord. What are your personal devotions like? What are you reading in the Bible these days? What are some answers to prayer you've received recently? When was the last time you shared your faith with an unbeliever? What sins are you struggling with right now in your life? What is the cutting edge of your spiritual life? Where are you growing? Where is God dealing with you?

Praying the Lord's Prayer (Mat. 6:9-13). This "Lord's Prayer," or the "Disciple's Prayer," was inspired and paraphrased by John Kenneth King, and is the way the prayer looks to a super committed cross-cultural worker:

"Praying in ordinary words, we have this wonderful example: Father, how could you trust us to take up the battle? The Dragon is here, waging war against those who are obeying your commandments and holding on to Jesus' testimony. We see that our struggle is not against human beings but against spiritual forces in high places here on earth.

Please carry out your kingdom, advance through us. Transform us from sleepy Christian clubs into delta strike forces. Please give us a clear sense of how long this battle has been going on and how many have entered the fray. Let us see ourselves as standing with Joseph and Mary against the powers that be. Produce a faith in us that knows the enemy cannot succeed against your Son.

Praise God! Jesus reigns! He does rule the nations with an iron scepter. He is there at your right hand, right now. You protected him until the perfect moment. He kept saying, "It is not my time…" until it finally arrived.

Please give us the clarity to realize the battles that are raging around us. Let us never rest in our fight against Satan and his angels. Use our testimony to overcome Him. Make your salvation and power—kingdom authority manifest among us. You've cast him down from heaven, and he no longer accuses us there. We praise You!"

(Note the power and, yes, the testimony of our Lord is more than worthy of action. It is our only lifeline in cross-cultural ministry and, yes, the sustenance of our very lives.)

Chapter 18

Was Paul a Cross-Cultural Minister of the Lord?

Paul is usually seen as the most obvious cross-cultural worker, as he went to the Mars Hill area to speak to the Athenians. What an incoherent question to even question his cross-cultural credentials! This apostle of Christ was the most prolific theologian and writer in the New Testament, who was fully a Jew and fully committed to reaching out to Gentiles.

Studying Paul in-depth reveals something encouraging to us, to all pastors and all Christians. We looked in depth at the significance of enculturation, as practiced by Jesus and the Samaritan "woman at the well." I'm ready to say, "Wow, I think I could do this as well!" Many of you know this method we have called enculturation. It came to my attention when a young man called Prince became a part of our church in Paris which Evey, my wife, and I planted to be an English/French church of 70 people. Prince followed me around like my personal disciple. He is from Sri Lanka and speaks Tamil and, of course, English.

My encouragement to him was to teach him how to reach other Sri Lankans to Christ. To do this, I went with Prince to visit Tamil homes. One home wanted to invite me for lunch. I was honored. But no one else was seated, just myself. They brought out a plate full of delicious food. As is quite typical in Sri Lankan, when an honored guest arrives, they prepare food for the visitor with one catch. As I ate the meat, a woman stood next to me and served me more meat. When I ate the potatoes, the woman standing next to me served me another helping of potatoes. I had a dinner valet. Such are the amazing parts of Sri Lankan culture.

We helped Prince when his wife had a baby from another father, unknown to Prince until sometime later. The sorrow and suffering Prince went through as his wife filed for divorce was unbearable. Yet as my disciple, he clung to every word of hope in God. I encouraged Prince to gather Sri Lankans to end up with a new church plant. I did what is called enculturation with Prince. I do not speak Sri Lankan and would not want to plant such a church and have a translation into Sri Lankan if Prince can do the job. This is exactly what Jesus did with the Samaritan woman in John 4. He coached her to become a Jesus follower, after which she led the whole town to Christ as Lord.

Was I acting cross-culturally? Yes, but more exactly, I was enculturating Prince to grow and reach into his own culture and be a sort of midwife to him. He went to England and entered a seminary and felt well-trained to have theological understanding under his belt. This was what I did with other converts from Islam as well.

Note clearly that I am not putting down Paul's methods or what he did as he possibly acted out enculturation. If it is this power to act as Paul did, every pastor and every Christian should look at this as an entry point to true cross-cultural enculturation.

But let's look a Paul more carefully. Was Paul truly a quintessential cross-cultural worker or not? The reality is that either in terms of gifting or strategic effectiveness or both, most of us will probably be more effective in a catalytic role like Barnabas than Paul. Maybe instead of aspiring to be like Paul, we should aspire to be like Barnabas and look for "Sauls" to help make into "Pauls" (especially if we're living in radically cross-cultural or multi-linguistic situations.)

Read these verses to really understand the significance of Barnabas, the Son of Encouragement:

Acts 4:36,37 35	Acts 15:1,2, 12
Acts 9:27 35-39	Acts 15:22-26,
Acts 11: 22-30	Gal. 2:1,13
Acts 12: 25	1 Cor. 9: 6
Acts 13: 1-3; 6-13; 42-52	Col. 4: 10
2 Tim. 4: 11	Acts 14: 11-20

What can you discern about Barnabas' character? What are the key roles that Barnabas played?

Some of the things you may discover character we should EMULATE:

Full of the Spirit

Respected

Humble

Generous

Credible

Willing to Travel

Not a complainer

"a good man" and "a dear friend"

Discerning

Equipper

Quick to Repent

Daily Letting His Heart be Godly

**Some of the things you may discover about Barnabas'
role that we can DO:**

Fast, pray, worship

Take risks on scary people (Paul)

Sacrifice our own ministry for others

Connect key people from one city to another (Antioch)

Travel to preach, connect, encourage, appoint elders, bring
aid

Advocate for Key People

Model ministry to others, including teaching and
preaching

See and develop others' potential and capacity

Evaluate and discern movements

Encourage faithfulness in others

Share authority

Work for cash when necessary to keep going

Give a 2nd chance to people (John Mark)

Submit as much as possible and be respectful to leaders

Disciple and mentor others (John Mark, Paul, and others)

Remarkable and Unexpected Elements in Enculturation

1. Start with Creation along with Christ. Show how Christ is the Living Word from even before the creation of the world. "In the beginning was the Word, and the Word was with God, and the Word was God. He was with God in the beginning. Through him, all things were made; without him, nothing was made that has been made. In him was life, and that life was the light of all humankind. The light shines in the darkness, and the darkness has not overcome it. (John 1:1-5)." Notice the order in the Word where Jesus was with God before the world was ever created. He is the Living Torah, as my Jewish Christian friends say.

2. Discover and obey is the goal, not teaching and knowledge. Jesus told parables but would not usually interpret them. Obedience is the key to being known by God, called by God, and enmeshed with Jesus as our Lord. Group accountability and group discovery take more time, but the result is not mass marketing. Knowledge will follow if God permits

3. Disciple people to conversion, not vice versa. This is to disciple the non-converted. This is reminiscent of Michael, the guitarist who I permitted to join our worship team, though the Bulgarian was not yet converted. However, he was very sympathetic and willing to follow Jesus. We call people to repentance, learn the sacrifice in the blood of

118

Jesus, baptism, and finally, discipleship. We choose the ordinary, who know nothing, and ask them to emulate the life Jesus lived.

4. Some heard the parables of Jesus and just went home and didn't care anymore. Others sang about the man who built his house on the rock, realizing that the rock is not just the Word of God but obedience to the Lord. The context also is the Rock who followed the children of Israel in the desert, Jesus Himself.

5. Encourage them to seek miracles. If miracles occur, you may need to skip to the story of Jesus, the miracle worker, and then come back to the creation and then back to the Old Testament. Many North Africans have come to Christ through reading Genesis 1-3, as the Father spoke clearly to sinful Adam and Eve, who clothed themselves in shame after sinning. Many have come to Christ by reading the genealogies of the New Testament.

6. Surprisingly, hostile and aggressive third-world people come to the Lord fast when the church in their midst is tepid and timid. Why? It is because the cross-cultural worker will not really put new converts into tepid churches but to start new fellowships in power and discipleship.

In Mauritania, there is an exceptional mosque where the Imam sends all his Islamic members to our Jesus follow teams to lead them all to Christ and baptize them. They return to the mosque as converted Muslims who carry their Bibles back to the mosque, all 200 of them. The Imam will not convert to Christ since he wants to maintain his link with other Imams. We call this a miraculous mosque because it is a place with the Spirit of the Lord all over the newly converted attendees. With all the work we do as cross-cultural leaders, the Imam has functioned as

Paul, the key person for enculturating people in the ways of Jesus the Lord.

Prayer, The Most Important Part of Enculturation, Puts God Beyond Our Methods

1. Train new Christians to pray. We shouldn't teach them to pray.

2. As you speak with an ethnic person, don't just pray for them, but pray together. Ask them to pray for you on the street. Give them words: "God, help Don," for example. Pray for Assimah, who needs help with her homework. Give her words, "Help Don to obey Jesus."

3. Ask if they have pain or suffering—then pray.

4. Ask if they have sorrow—then pray.

5. Pray for their religious leader if they follow one, even if he is hated or perverse.

6. Prayer walk in sectors of your community. Walk in 2s or 3s. Do spiritual scanning. Sense spiritual darkness. Name it and pray against it in Jesus' name.

7. Some of your team may fast during the daylight hours.

8. Pray for a person of peace, the person mentioned many times above, who is a person recognized with influence in the community. This corresponds to Barnabas' and Paul's enculturation, even as Jesus met with the Samaritan woman in John 4.

9. Model prayer in your church groups, don't just teach it.

10. When transcultural people find out that we are praying for them, they flood with joy. Prayer is so well-received

by modern, postmodern, and non-religious people that they don't see it as a religion to "bow to."

11. Don't be bound by the call for only men to speak with men, and women only speak to women. Paul had a vision from God wherein a man was calling for Paul to go to Macedonia to help his group. When Paul went there (Acts 16:14), he rather met a woman. "Now, a certain woman named Lydia heard us. She was a seller of purple from the city of Thyatira, who worshipped God. The Lord opened her heart to heed the things spoken by Paul." This man of peace was actually a woman of peace who was again an enculturation example as she planted a church, fully out of the norm for what Paul had expected. Paul was a God-listener, a catalyst to others, and one quick to obey God's calling.

12. Most movements to Christ start as prayer movements. No vision, no angelic visitation can in itself lead a person to Christ without the Word of God being spoken or read. We remember that Jesus is the Word that existed before the creation of the world.

13. Spiritual scanning, as noted above, can be in one region, in one home, or in one building. After visiting a household three times, you can ask if you could be allowed to clean the entire house of dark influences if the person accepts that it is done in the power of Jesus. You do not want to be known as the guru or shaman who has a special power. Jesus must be given the glory. If the person's home remains among the unconverted, the darkness may return with dire consequences seven times worse.

14. I have had spiritual leaders from various religions shout at me at a distance of 5 cm or 2 inches from my mouth. I took it in stride since all cultures have what is

called spacial metrics, which may widely differ from our own. In Western cultures, a spacial closeness metric of 2 inches means either love or anger.

15. Coach family groups. A single person won to Christ can be rejected much easier than an entire family that has a Bible and a Christian commitment.

16. Tell Bible stories that are understandable to kids and to the literate. Literates and illiterates need stories. Ask what the story means. Have them repeat it in their own words. What can they obey in the story? Next week, ask them to repeat the story that was read to them. Never tell them what conclusions to draw.

17. Mix compassion with empathy and prayer. Ask whoever needs prayer for healing or friendship, and bring them a small, hot meal, if possible, or a bag of fruit. This avoids coaching and telling but encourages being part of the family and their needs.

How Important Is Your Leadership In Cross-cultural or Enculturation?

I was fired twice by two former mission groups. But it set me free. In Acts 15, Paul was hauled before the council, who asked: "Why do you baptize before circumcising converts?" Change the thinking we have from 'I deserve everything to I have to why can't I choose the manner in which I die?' We have to choose to be faithful. A spiritual cross-cultural leader is the first to lose, the first to live, and the first to love. I am today through what I have walked through. When you take Isaac off the altar, by surrendering your leadership role or follower role in cross-cultural work, you are taking yourself off the altar too. We express fear from a passive outlook. Many of our churches are filled with fringe people who will not affect their cultures or any other culture but are wired just for themselves in isolation. Millions of people are waiting for you. Can you change their outlook and outcome of life? Are you the one, and have you come with the nations crying out?

How To Choose Leaders?

True cross-cultural leaders exhibit the fruit of the Spirit before they exhibit gifts of the Spirit. Timothy had Paul build up the fruit of his spirit. Timothy already had great spiritual gifts. Before a leader in China can lead a Christian house group, they have to have led 10 or 15 people to Christ. We know that leading people to Christ is the #1 cause of persecution. Mentors observe new believers through one cycle of persecution. The family of God determines their family. If kicked out of a house, they live with you. Remember, in Andrew Brunson's church, disciplers lived in the very homes of those whom they were discipling during a period of 90 days, monitoring the disciple every day, infusing them with the life of Jesus.

Oral Leadership

New ethnic believers are usually 83% oral—not all illiterate—in their effective and real means of communication or are functionally illiterate. They need to know what the Bible says. Westerners need to hear a story 7x to absorb it. Oral communicators need to hear a story 1x to absorb it. Jesus read from a text 1x. The rest of Jesus' words were to re-create an understanding of God's Old Testament by memory. It is likely that new ethnic believers will be unable to read or write, albeit in a limited way.

Oral tools are situation stories which are the best. They ask a question, and you can respond with a Bible story.

God keeps His word in oral forms to spread the transmission of His word. God keeps His word in literate forms to preserve the truth. Jesus did not use Scripture in anything but in oral forms. Remember that Jesus is the Living Word, the Living Torah, which existed before the creation of the world.

Let's summarize two very important conclusions. First, being in the model of Barnabas, we can use enculturation to motivate a man of peace like Paul. We have this as a piece of leverage that is undeniable from the story of Jesus and the Samaritan woman to Paul and Lydia, seeking to be simply a catalyst.

The second bright spark that we can stand upon is the fact that most oral peoples, that is, non-Western peoples, will know the stories after just one reading. We really need seven times to plunge into the Word to be radically changed. I think we are on to something.

Chapter 19

Twenty Churches Were Formed Before Western Isa (Jesus) Followers Arrived In Algeria

Amina is the strategist. She is able to listen to the flow of people and to enquire about how peoples move. She is a strong believer in knowing the underground plans of people and how they fit into her thoroughly engrained apocalyptic view of ISIS Islam. She will talk with Muslims, Isa's followers, the police, the army, and the business leaders and college students in Algerians. I left her alone for a week to come back to me and to give me a report on her findings in a land that was very strange to her. She traveled hundreds of kilometers, taking buses, flying taxis, staying in hotels and living with Isa followers, and learning the jigsaw puzzle of the flow of the movement of Isa followers. She came back with a dossier and drawings and plans and vector arrows of movements that astonished me.

Her report pretty much could have pushed me over with a leaf. She took names, strategies, and places. Here is her report.

Amina reported,

"First, there are Isa followers all over Algeria that are not part of a church. They are isolated and looking for leadership. Along come Farid, Farhad, and Mogul, who visited the Kabyles and Tuaregs in Tamanrasset.

"Second, they are motivated to go out from Kabila so as not to be a burden to their families. This element of honor to their parents gives Kabyle Isa followers the motivation to leave home and travel afar to speak about Isa to everyone they meet.

"Third, the Kabyle method is not argumentative, as would be the highly educated Imams who have strings and strings of arguments. In fact, at times, Kabyles grab people by the collar of the shirt and tell them that they must believe that Isa is the son of God. Under pressure, the poor Muslim says yes, and then violently gets pulled into a Holy Bible study and prayer. They become Isa's followers. The offspring of Kabyle followers of Isa has an inner violence that is dedicated to Isa, whom they call the son of God.

"Fourth, they send out swarms of Kabyle Isa follower teachers who just tear through places like Biskra, Constantine, Anaba, Alwat, Tiaret, and Amusaret. Rachid and Hamid lead a team of 36 that swarm like locusts through these and other towns.

"Most remarkably, and most outlandishly, and most shockingly, churches are formed in towns and cities before followers of Isa arrive. You heard me right. This is a development that puts shivers up my spine. How can this be? What happens is that a single Isa follower announces to other Muslims that a team of Isa followers are coming to town. They, along with their trusted Muslim friends, build or rent a building for a church in anticipation of the event of a swarm of Isa followers soon to arrive.

"The church building awaits the movement of Isa's followers to fill it. One man calls all the Muslim sympathizers to build or rent the building like a ceremonial tent is raised up to welcome a dignitary to town.

"The only way I can see breaking this spiral of sympathizers is to create a band of Muslim clerics and Imams that bring people toward Islam in a greater way through informers, erecting Sharia law, punishing those missing from the mosque, and those who have not paid alms and gone to Mecca for the Hajj. We need to shower the need for Sharia law to stop the flaunted approach to bring shame upon the Religion and upon Allah."

Another letter to Farid,

Nabil here. We have a remarkable ally in my wife Amina. She has studied the entire Algerian underground system among followers of Isa. The results are not flattering. We are carrying a shitload of trouble in this nation where all our efforts are relying on a just visiting Isa followers.

The Isa followers are miles ahead of us. Short of an invasion of clerics, Imams, and the introduction of monitors and the movement toward punishment and Sharia law to reinforce the shame and dishonor brought to the Religion and to Allah.

I have the right person in Amina, Farid. She, as a strategist, has found that these shrewd followers of Isa have used the Islamic principle of honor to not burden their parents. This releases them to form swarms of teachers to coerce Muslims into being followers of Isa.

They have visions and churches set up before the churches have any followers of Isa in the area. Can you believe this? I'm so pissed off that we have to babysit these Muslims to make them stand up as fundamentalists. The start of the Talibe training was severe and strong. Then drifting into peace with the Isa followers cursed and weakened the Religion. Where is the Hajj? Who goes to Mecca now?

Where are the bombers who follow the Koran to eliminate the Isa followers and the pornographic Western nations? The hate in my heart has to be poured out to bring balance to the world I live in that is out of balance. So dishonor has to be restored, or else my life and Amina's life will be flooded with the jinn/demons. We are dishonored and need the shame lifted from our lives to keep on living. Soon it will be clear that dishonor before Allah is what we have now.

Enlarging The Spy Family

My trip to Raqqa provided more than insight into the blueprint for the Sharia to be imposed by ISIS on Algeria. Nor was the interrogation the full intent of the meeting and the subsequent tour of captive women. My encounter with Hayat was enough to first drain my facial expression to ash. But then, there was much more than a renewal for me to set me back on course.

I found a 24-year-old Al-Khansa member that was an extremely wonderful and appealing young woman. Sergeant Amina had destroyed or kidnapped 100s of kidnapped women. I took her aside one night and asked her to follow me to Algeria to enlarge my team and become my wife. Passing through the Imam and the council of ISIS, it was agreed that ISIS would function better with Amina on my right arm.

Her background is Syrian, with the dark, beautiful almond-shaped eyes and the fierceness of a Muslim who would die a Muslim, and no other way. She had her parents destroyed by Assad's barrel bombs and then became adopted by ISIS as a point of safety for herself. That is, she became the woman of pleasure for returning ISIS fighters, as were many others captured, and promised one way to stay alive, by being a woman in waiting.

She began to organize the brothel with such administrative and tyrannical passion for ISIS that she was promoted after being tested by beheading Isa's followers and Iraqi fighters. Her turning point was that she felt that the Koran could only be understood by following "death to infidels" in order to fight to become welcomed into the caliphate and, at the end of time, to fight in the plains of Syria. Death was expected, and giving torture and death to others was all part of bringing in the apocalyptic end of the world. Death was simply a pathway for her, a conveyor belt to put others onto as they await the Shiite equivalent of the return of the Mahdi.

Beautiful Amina, part of the Al-Khansa forever, became my bride, my lover, and my co-strategist in Algeria. I told Farid that we have the power of ten, being unable to slow our pursuit of the expansion of Isa's followers. ISIS also felt that a couple would have more cover in the work of espionage in Algeria. I swell with pride to have a member of the Al-Khansa brigade on my mission.

However, I am not a man without a memory. I cannot forget the Holy Bible and the reading by Hayat that Allah does want to associate with human beings. I have all the power of strategy and the spirit of death but ridden with fear that if Allah would associate with human beings, he could somehow be condemned for His strategy. That gives me two strategy options, the one read by Hayat and the death wish of Al-Khansa Amina. No, life is not resolved by lying in the bosom of my wife. This I cannot share with Amina. But, with Farid and Amina, and myself, ISIS has at least a presence in Algeria.

We heard about a very suffering and downcast Arab woman, Naaisha, who was reading her Koran in Batna, Algeria, south of Constantine and south of Setif. Then, enter a Kabyle woman. The Kabyle woman's daughter was healed by Allah/God in a matter of minutes. This miracle changed Naaisha, who is now an outspoken front liner for other Arab, Kabyle, and Chawi women as well.

Here's the story. First of all, Naaisha was given an Arabic Bible by the Kabyle woman, crossing into another culture to do so. Naaisha hid it. When we visited her, we could tell the Holy Bible hadn't been touched. But as we prayed for her, Allah answered prayer in very specific ways. So she began to go to the Holy Bible and read the Koran at the same time. Now when we visit Naaisha, she brings the Holy Bible out, even without being asked.

Then she said she had her first dream of Isa. The result was that she wanted to share Isa with her sister. In still another dream, her cancer-ridden sister was told by Isa that He was healing the sister. She comes to all church meetings, and she prays. She had the gris-gris, doing all the witchcraft, and cleaned out her house of these talismans. She is different inside and out. This month is her first Ramadan, and sparks will fly. She has no one in her family, though she is quite fearful of what her family with think of her if she doesn't do Ramadan. She will either do Ramadan as a point of ummah solidarity or avoid it to be free of the twilight of jinn/demonic activity, from which she is, according to her, now protected by Isa/Jesus.

Amina and I decided to visit her in Batna, where hospitality is always present among "Muslims." So they will receive us. It took three bus trips, so I hoped it was going to be a strong visit with Naaisha. The buses in Algeria stop at each house to drop off each passenger at their door since everything else is on foot. We had the address, and off we went.

Arrival at Naaisha's home was like going through a veil of spirits, which was very uncomfortable for us. We were only to find that Naaisha attended a newly formed church of 200 people in Batna. We were not just talking to a leading woman, but with the prayer and multi-cultural word bearer of Isa from her whole church.

We were immediately invited into Naaisha's home with a place to eat and lodge for the night. Our commission wasn't to change her ways of thinking but to try to locate the basis of the expansion of this Isa movement. It would be hard. She may have lies and tall tales that prove her indoctrination. I'm just hoping for someone who doesn't have this voyeurism to pronounce a curse on us and to bare us our true intentions. I couldn't let Amina see this since she has no concept of the spiritual world yet. She might reach out and assassinate Naaisha in a hurry. Amina is slightly robotic and trained, with much blood on her hands. Being in front of an infidel is one thing. Being with an Isa follower may drive her to kill. I was sure that some danger awaited us. Can Amina be so brainwashed that she will kill on command or kill on some external prompt or fear? Amina was astonishingly strong and passionate.

We had a light supper of Algerian foods, Hallel chicken, boiled eggs, cucumber, and boiled eggs, served with gunpowder and mint tea. She made tea in a way that lifted the teapot two meters off the table and filled our narrow tea glasses three times after putting them back into the teapot. Sugar was in abundance.

The morning came early, with roosters and goats and donkeys sounding off to welcome the day. Naaisha, we asked the following: How Isa's followers came to form a church of 200. She responded,

"Are you with the government to trouble us?"

No, no, rather learn how to bring Muslims together as Isa's followers and to gather them into a church. Are you funded by the West? Are you an apostate Muslim? Have you renounced the name of Mohammed, be praised?

"I see you are still Muslims. But you are welcome in our home and church. Everyone in our church has had hours of prayer and consequential visions of Isa, who called them to His side. More than visions, we are bound together by obedience to Isa, who calls us to tell of His name everywhere we go. The Holy Bible calls us to be healers and not killers."

What about all the years of Islamic culture that are preparing you for an eternity with Allah?

"Nabil, you know that there is no place for Muslim women before Allah or before men except the bedroom. Besides, I'm free of the curses of the Islamic world, which casts jinn/demons upon us daily. I'm not putting my culture before or in place of Isa. Tell me if you want to meet other members or other Isa followers."

Farid, as you know, I am now married and stronger with a member of the brigade of Al-Khansa, Amina, an ISIS sergeant. She just had her first encounter with a follower of Isa and kept her cool. We are both worried since we realize that we need to come with ISIS in masse. These Isa followers are not only dispersed, but they cross cultures from Kabyle to Chawi to Arab. Empirical evidence of healings and heavenly visions are calling them to read their Holy Bibles.

The culture of Islam is not sufficiently powerful to keep all Muslims from the filthy change of becoming western and infidels and followers of Isa, remembering that the police in Algeria and the army are now copying the ways of GIA and the Afghan fighters of the 1990s. We are faced with diversified Isa followers and highly committed government officials who would repel any large invasion of ISIS fighters. It may be our only hope to help become race baiters and to turn the national population of Muslims against what we can portray as fledgling Isa followers who are undermining the great nation of Algeria.

Amina can kill but is holding back as a strategist. There is some way to turn anti-Isa sympathizers against the Isa followers and to make the government and the army money or strategy to wipe out these Isa followers. We may get out of here and head for the far south to Tamanrasset. Notify Al-Khansa in Raqqa that Amina is strong and easily adapting to this situation but holding fire for the purpose of a larger strategy. She is a key Muslim player, and I trust her judgment since she obeys me as a Muslim wife must obey.

Epilogue

There is no greater call than to meet people cross-culturally outside our comfort zone. The result is that our comfort zone enlarges to move from cross-cultural ministry to inter-cultural ministry, which keeps us from isolating an ethnic person to a person who feels far a part of your culture too.

It doesn't stop there. Enculturation was set before us with the stories of Jesus and the Samaritan woman and likewise with Barnabas and Paul. In each case, we see how a person of peace can be catalyzed so they can run with the calling in Christ to make disciples. It turns the traditional fear on its head of reaching one person at a time to empowering and enculturing the catalytic person. But our role of being a Barnabas continues not by giving all the answers as the "Bible answer man or woman," but

133

encouraging new groups in their search to reach out to still others as they share within their cultural boundaries and beyond.

This book has not withheld the reality of the dark powers which oppose not only cross-cultural ministry but all who are moving beyond their cultural cocoon. Darkness may arrive from our own cultural pressure to conform to secularism or even as teams of militants who seek to prey on our Christian values, as the true stories from Algeria and Somalia prove pernicious to God's people who never gave up. The good news is that Jesus is the light, and the darkness has not overcome His Light and our light as we walk in faithfulness to Him. "In him was life, and that life was the light of all humanity. The light shines in the darkness, and the darkness has not overcome it. (John 1:4,5)" Remember Naaisha and her faithfulness and unfailing devotion to proclaim Christ to all in power and kindness. Jesus is your light, your master, and your life. Go and proclaim Him.

How to Use This Book

Over the years, I have launched church-wide cross-cultural seminars. This has taken place in a dozen churches in various denominations and states in the USA. This book adds a fuller understanding of cross-culturalism that goes beyond the 1-, 2-, or 3-day seminars. My contact for further information and a possible seminar in your church is hdonparis@gmail.com I live in France and hold seminars in September and October every year. Join us in the fun of knowing more of God's kingdom and your potential to serve Him. Our website is PraxisAdvocates.com Honor is given to Greg Livingstone, Bruce Graham of Frontier Ventures,unk and Erik Aasland for their inspiration for this book.

Made in the USA
Monee, IL
03 July 2023

38553644R00075